THE BUSINESS PSYCHIC

The Business Psychic

VANESSA JONES

Contents

Chapter 1

Chapter 1

Ruby had an icky feeling in her tummy the second she saw him walk through the security gates and into Grayson's Bookstore. His appearance seemed benign enough but there was something in the way his almost grey hair flopped about and the daggy khaki dad shorts that he was sporting that put her on alert.

It wasn't her usual shift at the bookstore but she wanted to take what she could, considering her finances were less than optimal at the moment. Or, at any moment in history to be more accurate. Besides, she owed her work buddy, Cooper, a favour after he covered for her last time when she was running late because she'd spent the morning trying to negotiate an extension on her already way too overdue to admit phone bill. She threw up some threats about leaving the company and going to their competitor, to which the person on the other end of the phone just laughed at her and said, 'ma'am, at this point you are a liability to us so you can go where you like.'

Cooper was unassuming and pretty. His flawless skin caused some stares and some envy and he had a calmness that was almost palpable. His honey flecked hair was always so artfully styled with a deep sweeping fringe that anyone would be jealous of.

Ruby just loved being near him because he seemed so together, so relaxed and by being next to him she could feel herself soaking up his vibes. For someone who was considerably younger than her 32 years, he was so much more mature. Ruby hadn't once met any of his boyfriends, although he divulged their entire relationship history and backstory any time she'd ask and it just added to the air of mystery that he so effortlessly portrayed. One which he denied he even had every time Ruby prodded him to reveal more about himself.

Ruby remembered the first time she met Cooper. He'd been working at the bookstore quite a few months before she came in for her trial shift. He looked at her with disdain when she walked in, a damp sheen from the light misty rain outside covering her face and hair. Ruby told herself that it was probably her age and her total lack of prospects that arose off her aura and everywhere she went and put him off. She was used to putting people off, just for existing. The scary part was that she was not only getting used to it but was getting comfortable with it.

During that first shift, the two were left alone in the store, not saying a word to one another. Ruby silently hoped that no customer would come in as she had no idea what to do and Cooper did not seem the type to help her. She busied herself with a duster and reshelving books, learning the unusual layout of the place. The nonfiction hiding all the way in the back corner, whilst the fiction was split in two parts making it extremely hard for anybody to find what they were looking for. Or what they weren't looking for but probably needed.

In the centre of the shop, about a metre from the door a round display table was erected, which was always piled with books to form an uneven pyramid. Often, it was comprised of popular sellers or something that the owner, Murray, had accidentally over-ordered and want to get rid of in a hurry. The usual *Fifty Shades* or Dan Brown whatnots. Once, Murray hit 1000 instead of 10 on an order of a small hardback which exclusively featured interviews with glassblowers across the globe. So ever since then, there was always a pile of *Glassblowers International* on that central pyramid that never seemed to diminish. There were also several boxes of the title out the back, taking up space and causing a trip hazard that made Ruby furious.

During that first shift, Ruby accidentally swiped the corner of the table with her curvaceous hip, knocking an armful of books to the floor. Her face flushed red and hot and she shook slightly as she looked down at the books splayed before her. Mentally kicking herself for her awkwardness, she held her hands up and announced that 'shit like Kerouac is better off on the floor anyway. Perfect place for it.' Her hands flew to her mouth as she realised what she had said out loud. Looking to Cooper with even deeper embarrassment, she noticed him giggling to himself. A silent giggle barely jostled his shoulders. But it was there.

Instantly, Ruby relaxed and the tension in her body flew away. For the rest of the shift, she didn't feel the need to walk on eggshells although they hardly spoke. When it came time for Ruby to finish her shift and leave, she boldly walked by Cooper, high fived him and said, 'I'll see you tomorrow old friend.' And swaggered out.

Cooper gradually warmed to her over the following week and by the weekend, they were close enough to be labelled friends. Their friendship had been consistent and reliably codependent ever since.

Ruby thought about her favourite, and only, friend Cooper. The way his hair hung straight from a perfectly formed side part that made you want to trail your finger down it. And his blue eyes that were icy at the best of times, which didn't entirely match his demeanour. He was stoic but, as Ruby discovered quickly, he was quite warm and always thoughtful. More than once he would bring her little succulent offcuts from his garden, planted into a floral teacup to jazz up her apartment's décor. And anytime he went and bought a coffee, he automatically got her one too. Even when it was late in the afternoon when she repeatedly told him that she didn't drink coffee after one because it kept her awake at night. 'It's not about drinking the coffee,' he told her. 'It's about the gesture.'

'Oh and I love the gesture,' Ruby swept her hands over her chest in a melodramatic fashion. 'I wish a distant relative would cark it and gesture a million dollars into my bank account. Like tomorrow. Tonight would be handier.'

Cooper would always tuck his chin down and grin his trademark grin anytime Ruby attempted to be funny. Even when she, admittedly, was reaching.

In contrast to Cooper's distinctive Eastern European look— Ruby thought she remembered him saying that his grandparents were from Hungary— she looked almost the opposite. If they were colours, Cooper would be white and Ruby would be, well she would be Ruby like her namesake.

The sharpness of her eyebrows, unfortunately, made her seem more interested in what people were telling her than she actually was and it caused Cooper to often mildly chide her when she'd question, 'why do people always tell me their whole life story?'

'Well stop acting like you give a damn and they might find another victim. Be like me, constant deadpan. People think I can't even understand them. That's how blank my face is. You can only aspire to be the level of blank-faced that I am! Someone should make a documentary about my face. *The Legend of the Deadpanned Man*. Ninety minutes run time. Soon, kids all over the country will be looking in the mirror practising limp facial expressions. It will be a hoot.'

'It would certainly be something.'

After a bit, he said 'Hey, thanks again for taking this shift for me, Ruby.' Cooper reached across the counter he was leaning on and squeezed her hand jolting her out of her reverie about their friendship. 'My theatre thing is just really giving me back a bit of my confidence.'

'Oh seriously, it's the least I can do for you. And, you know, the whole need-more-money thing.'

'Still no luck on getting those bills sorted, eh?'

'Somehow it feels like they are slipping more and more out of control and away from me. I wish I could stop time for a bit, you know? Catch up.'

'Ew. Time seems to drag well enough, thank you.' Cooper looked at a row of books thoughtfully and hesitated before turning back to Ruby.

'I'm not trying to be a jerk here but...'

'Said every person right before being an utter jerk,' Ruby joked.

'If you're still this broke, how on earth are you ever going to afford to buy this place if it comes up for sale?'

Ruby sighed. All she'd ever wanted was to own her own bookstore, not just work in one. And the ideas that she had for this place would often keep her awake at night. 'Well, that's exactly the point. Thanks for bursting my daydream.' The till slammed shut a little harder than necessary.

'I'm not trying to razz you, honestly. I'm just curious about your plan. You're always playing the victim card but I haven't seen you take steps to change it.' Cooper tucked his bottom lip underneath his top and Ruby could see tiny sweat beads pop up and rim his neck. It must have taken him a lot of courage to be this bold and confront her like this. Normally, their friendship was based on that of gentle codependency and constant reassurance that each other were doing the right thing. Ruby felt immediately affronted by Cooper's accusation.

'You think I'm playing a victim?' She unconsciously held up the pricing gun and tapped it against her cheek as if it were a real handgun.

'I didn't mean it like that. I meant... I don't know. I'm sorry. Just forget I said anything. I'm nervous about my theatre group.'

'Right,' she said unconvinced.

'I'll just shelve this last lot of books and

then head off. It shouldn't be too busy today so you'll be fine on your own.'

'Yes, I'm sure I will be but it will be boring as maths without you here to keep me company.'

'Flattered.' Cooper grabbed an armful of wayward books and wafted like a silent ghost to the floor to ceiling shelves carefully placing one by one back in their rightful spot.

After a few minutes of silence, he announced he was leaving. 'I'm off then Ruby.'

'So when are you going to tell me more about your play? Is it *Hamilton*? Or *Les Mis*? Please tell me it's neither of those because I just don't think I could sit through either no matter how much I love you.' Ruby had already forgiven him for pulling her up on her financial woes.

Cooper blushed and said 'it's neither but it's a surprise.'

'Tease! Surely you'd want some character tips from someone as naturally melodramatic as me? You on tomorrow?'

'Yep, see you then.'

'Have fun repeatedly saying "Yes, and..."

'That's improv. Thankfully we don't do that.'

'Oh but you have done it though, right?' Ruby said cheekily as she imagined a circle of thin theatre geeks throwing an imaginary ball between one another.

'Why YES I have. AND you have fun working.'

Ruby smiled a genuine heartfelt smile at his back as he slung his satchel over his shoulder and slid out the front door, in his vampire-esque way. Teasing him, she would often call him 'Edward' after a certain young adult series they both hated but still sold by the box load. Her life was basically crumbling around her thanks to her financial stress but around Cooper, she felt genuinely happy. The reflection of the back of the door shone an image of herself back at her. Her auburn hair looked flat, she hadn't really given it the attention it needed to be impressive but at least she had time to put on a tinted moisturiser and a lip gloss. Ruby didn't consider herself stunning. She was pretty in the face. But her flagging self-esteem wouldn't allow her to think of herself in high regards, especially as she was convinced that her curvy body was the biggest detractor from everything she had to offer. 'I'm one of those girls that people say that I have a great personality,' she would laugh with Cooper. The subtext meaning that she was unattractive. 'If only they knew that my personality was lame as well.' Cooper would heartily disagree with her but she would laugh it off, knowing that the best way to deal with how she saw herself was to be the funny one.

When the middle-aged man who was stationed in the middle of the corner of coffee table books at the back of the store sneezed, Ruby jumped. She had forgotten he was there and was grateful that she hadn't let out a cheeky fart which she has been known to do when she has been all alone in Grayson's Bookstore, possibly her most favourite place that she has ever worked. The way she felt in bookstores was what she imagined people felt like going to church or sitting around playing computer games and smoking weed with friends. It was a comfort, blanket of familiarity and an exhilaration all at once. A beautiful cocktail of neurochemicals that made her feel alive and appreciative that she had found a tiny bit of a mecca in the city where she lived. Without a boyfriend or many friends and most of her family remaining back home in the small town where she grew up, there wasn't a lot of support around Ruby. And the small pocket of livelihood that the bookstore and Cooper provided her was worth the constant stress of trying to get her rent and bills paid, even if she had to be on that hamster wheel for a few more years.

What she really wanted to do was buy her own bookstore. Not just any bookstore but the one they both worked in. For she loved it like people loved church. A place that called her and opened her heart. Whenever she was in the belly of the Grayson's Bookstore, or indeed any bookstore, her skin relaxed and she felt held and comforted by an invisible force. After her dad left their family, Ruby grappled with a loneliness that no kid should ever have to experience. She had school friends and her mum was ever so devotional. But the void that was created by her father leaving for what seemed like no real reason to Ruby was so vast and perturbing that it infected every one of her days.

That was until she went to the library after

school one day when her mum was running late for school pickup. She intended just to pass the time but a kindly librarian spotted her and walked over to some shelves. Ruby will never forget the sound that her long denim skirt made, like a parachute cutting through the wind, as she strolled over and plucked out a book by its spine. Handing it to Ruby, she looked over her crimson glasses, which sat neither at the top or bottom of her nose and simply stated, 'you'll like this one.' And pointed her towards a pile of empty bean bags.

The librarian was right. Ruby loved the book so much that she read it overnight and the story stayed with her as an adult. Twice a week she would pay a visit to the library and get as many books as she was allowed to borrow at once. Mostly, the limit was four but if the librarian with the crimson glasses was feeling generous, she would allow Ruby an extra one. Escaping into the worlds that the books held was a true salve for her. In the books, the characters had full and rich lives and were rarely lonely. And if they were, they'd find a way to overcome it. Ruby never felt lonely when she was lost inside a story.

Books quickly became her medicine and she wanted to be able to be in complete control of dispensing it to those who deserved it as little Ruby did. Like some kind of bookstore pharmacist. But unless she won the lottery or stole a fair chunk of money, she wasn't really in a position to do that anytime soon. Ruby sighed with despondency as she recalculated how far away she was from her dream of owning the bookstore. It kept getting further and further away as her debts kept layering on top of themselves. Murray gave her as many shifts as he could and she had been working on him, laying the groundwork for suggesting they stay open a little later each night so she could work more. Every one of her shifts she went above and beyond with the hope that Murray would notice and give her a raise or, in the very least, praise her efforts. But, as they say, hope is a wasted thing. Nevertheless, it was important for Ruby to upkeep the maintenance of the shop and its reputation. Every shift she would sweep twice, keep the window display replenished and eye-catching and make informed recommendations to customers.

With one look, she could tell exactly what kind of book the customer would enjoy. It was her superpower. There were the harassed forty-something mothers that, whilst their makeup was flawless, they had tiny little bloodshot lines cracking through the whites of their eyes. Ruby would always suggest two books for them, without fail. A book to keep up appearances and impress their friends or colleagues, usually a literary classic or a stimulating biography that everyone was talking about. But she also made sure to balance it out with a fly-through read of something fun. A beachside romance or a *Da Vinci Code* or whatever was most popular with sixteen-year-olds at the time. Ruby could always feel the gratitude come off them as they swiped their Amex cards or tapped their phones at the counter. This was one of Ruby's best customer retention strategies as they were invariably back. Even if they didn't buy anything, they just loved to be seen by someone, anyone, even if it was the near-invisible Ruby. Without a shadow of a doubt,

Ruby knew that if she handed them a glass of sauvignon blanc and asked them how they were really doing, she'd have them liquefied into a puddle of tears within seconds. Perhaps being a therapist was on the cards? No Ruby, she shook her head at herself. Where would you get the money for the education?

Then there were the teenage customers. Surprisingly, they were an easy bunch and a joy for Ruby to help. Most of them knew exactly what they didn't and did want to read and, if they ventured into the bookstore, they were voracious readers. So the challenge was finding them something new and fresh that they hadn't yet read. It was a challenge that thrilled Ruby and she would keep aside a few special books every time a new box came in.

The wealthy customers were the ones that Ruby hated, but needed, the most. They spent so much and didn't particularly care what they were buying. It's almost as if they just wanted to offload some cash and thought that it was better to spend on books then on something untoward. But they kept the bookstores afloat with their frivolous and regular spending habits.

One such customer was Herman. Ruby had only ever seen him in the store once or twice before and both times Cooper had served him. She remembered Cooper saying to his back after he had left, 'that man has too much money. It makes him ugly.'

On this day, Herman was rifling through the nonfiction section in the back corner. She didn't feel particularly motivated to help him, assuming he would just spend some money anyway. She hoped that the after-school crowd would soon appear and she could be distracted by the exquisite gift of finding that perfect book. There was a new book by a new author that had just come in, complete with a dark violet cover that she knew a few regular teens would absolutely get a kick out of.

A sneeze ricocheted throughout the store, bringing Ruby back into the present.

'Sorry, I didn't mean to startle you with my old man sneeze,' the guy declared, hastily stuffing his handkerchief back into one of his many pockets. He tried a lazy smile at Ruby who couldn't help but notice his watery eyes were announcing that he was not in the least bit sorry for sneezing.

'No, it's totally fine. Can I help you find something?' She asked as chirpily as she could muster, whilst one part of her brain was still calculating how much money she now owed.

The man gestured towards a heaving shelf at his eye-line. 'I have all these. Do you have anything new out back or on its way?'

Ruby smoothed her hands down over her slate grey button-up work shirt as was a habit when she wanted to appear more professional in front of customers that weren't her regulars.

'No, I'm sorry all we have is on the shelf. Perhaps there's something I could special order in for you?' Ruby hated the sound of her customer service voice with its unnaturally grating perkiness. But she had learnt long ago that if you don't look like you are going above and beyond, even greeting a customer, they take it as a personal offence that you are being rude to them. And honestly, Ruby was far too self-obsessed to bother being rude to anyone.

The man stepped a little closer to Ruby and

leant across her towards a wide book on yachts of the world. She could smell his dusty deodorant waft up from under his arm, so she looked down, embarrassed. His toes were thick and weathered, poking out through some horrible reef sandals that she only ever saw toddlers and old dads wear. The man paused with his hand on the thick book spine and looked across to Ruby. She desperately wanted to get back to the safety of behind the counter but whilst he had his arm up, she was cornered between an overfull bookshelf and the man. Ruby knew, from experience, that if he moved too quickly and dislodged that heavy book, that it would drop squarely on her toe.

'Yeah actually...' Herman cleared his throat but didn't move his arm. 'How can I order one of you?'

Ruby's face fell and she searched his eyes for what she was hoping was a joke. An inappropriate joke but one nonetheless. But his face had morphed into that of a sleazy monster and she was sure that she hadn't misheard him and that the icky feeling that stuck in her gut from the moment he walked in was onto something.

He moved his hip across a little so she was even more hemmed in.

Ruby panicked and froze. She just kept hoping that he would move out the way so she could slip quietly back to the counter where she would feel safe enough to reject him or laugh him off. Being trapped like a mouse like this meant that Ruby knew she was vulnerable and her instinct was to get away at all costs.

'Excuse me?' Ruby said, prickly but quivering painfully on the inside. Her stomach gurgled and she suddenly badly needed to evacuate her bowels.

'You heard, dollface. I wanna spread you across my coffee table like these expensive books.' The deodorant smell increased threefold and clogged up the air. Ruby was worried it would taint the books.

'Uh, no... no thank you.' Ruby stammered out.

'Yes.' It was delivered so casually, so evenly that Ruby started to sweat. The skin underneath her nostrils and eye troughs became damp.

Without much more thought, Ruby looked

at the most exposed part of the man— his revolting round potbelly— and shoved an elbow in, whilst simultaneously lifting up her foot in case the book fell onto it as he retracted his arm to cradle his stomach. Leaving him hunched over, Ruby skittered away from him and straight into the back storeroom, where she locked the door behind her.

Panting, she dabbed at her face with tissues and double-checked that the door was locked. Continuing to repetitively dab at her face, long after any moisture was gone, she plonked herself in front of the three rectangular boxes that ran uninterrupted black and white footage. On the CCTV footage, she watched him as her nerves were on fire and as he crouched down for much longer than she wanted.

Looking around her and smacking down the side of her body, searching for pockets even though she had none, she realised that her phone was still under the bench of the counter on the other side of the door. But there was no way she was going to risk the haven of the locked room to grab it and call the police. Who would probably just laugh at her anyway. Just like the telephone company guy did. Would she be a liability to the police too?

After what seemed like an hour but was mere minutes, she watched Herman uncurl and hobble towards the front of the store on the screen, not before he threw a handful of cheap paperbacks across the counter, towards the storeroom door. The thud hit the door a split second before she saw it on the monitor and her nerves spiked up again.

As soon as Ruby heard the doorbell jingle and was sure he was gone, she careened out to the front of the shop and locked the door. Shaking she sunk down behind the counter, with one of the paperbacks that he'd thrown keeping her company. The book's cover had been damaged— a little tear an inch long at the bottom edge— and Ruby picked it up furiously because that meant that it wouldn't be able to be sold. She was more unreasonably mad that he'd ruined a book that could have been sold than she was about his attempt at... what? She said to herself. 'What was that exactly?'

Before she could define what happened to her, find a label that worked, her phone rang and interrupted the air. It was Murray, her boss. Murray was a warm man in his fifties that didn't really have a lot to do with the bookstore. He phoned occasionally with not much more than technical and practical information, such as '...the electrician will be in tomorrow at 10am'. He didn't really connect with her, or Cooper, keeping them both at a distance rather than befriending them. Which was fine with Ruby because it helped her to imagine that the bookstore was all her very own.

Answering the phone, a wash of relief passed through her and despite herself, she started crying. 'I've just had the most horrible experience with a customer and I...'

'Save it, Ruby. I've just had Herman phone me to tell me what disgusting treatment you gave one of our best customers. Do you know how much money he has spent with us over the years? He said you assaulted him!' Murray yelled, the phone vibrating in Ruby's hand.

'But I had to!'

'Ruby, there is no excuse for assaulting any-one. Let alone our best customer.' Her boss sounded so furious that she thought she could hear spittle leaping from his mouth and hitting the phone.

'But he tried to assault me!' Ruby was lost for words. She couldn't believe how this had been turned around on her but couldn't stop crying enough to form a cohesive defence.

'Ruby, I saw it on the footage. It looked very much like you assaulted him. Lock up the place now. I'm coming down to take over your shift in half an hour and I do not want you to be there. In fact, I don't want you in my shop ever again.'

Ruby was absolutely heartbroken. Fired for something that wasn't her fault! From a job she loved. As her eyes became so blurry from tears, she shoved her phone into her small backpack, picked up the books the man had flung and placed them neatly back on the display pyramid where they belonged.

She stepped out onto the footpath and locked the door behind her and reassured herself that she would be back. Surely, once Murray had time to think about things logically and see that she was merely defending herself from... she shuddered as her imagination tried to poke at her with scary scenarios of what could have unfolded.

'He'll change his mind.' She said to herself. 'I mean, he has to, how else am I going to keep paying these stupid bills.' The thought of not having a job with the financial pressure she was already under made her heave and sob. Thankfully, the street was busy with people bustling with their own problems and jobs or errands they had to get to and she could walk the few blocks to her drab apartment without anyone really noticing that she was crying herself into a dark spiral.

Chapter 2

Chapter 2

Chapter 2

After flinging herself on her bed, Ruby cried until she left two identical circles of tears the size of saucers on her doona. The geometric shapes of the doona cover stared demonstratively back up at her.

Glancing around her room, where she could easily see the front door from her bed, she grimaced at the grimness of it all. Two squeaky carrot coloured chairs either side of a flimsy wooden table that functioned as her dining table. A dusty tapestry couch that had matching holes in either arm and no curtains to block out the daylight and the winter's cold in the lounge room. Thankfully Ruby had no need or desire for a TV, even if she could afford one. Where ordinarily a TV would be, there were piles and piles of books stacked up against the wall. Every time she looked at them, she felt half elated and half sad that she couldn't even provide them with the dignity of a proper bookshelf. 'One day, my pretties,' she would say to them, patting them lightly as if they were dogs.

Ruby stumbled to the bathroom, wiped her tears on her towel and went into her tiny kitchen, which was basically a sink and a small fridge lined up against one wall, whilst the other end of the wall housed the couch. Flicking the kettle on, she pulled out one of the many mismatched mugs. Ruby couldn't believe she was even a person that would ever have matching mugs, not even cheap ones and it made her sad. As the water boiled, she looked over to the pile of letters that had been pushed inelegantly under her door. The pile filled her with dread and she knew what they said without even having to open then.

Every day now was just a waiting game until

she was asked to leave her apartment. In fact, Ruby had a sickening suspicion that that is exactly what one of those letters laying unattended to on her sticky kitchen linoleum said. And so, she cried some more. She cried at the injustice of being female when it's a woman's word against a man's and how shitty this whole society was still after all these centuries.

But mostly she cried because she lost a job she loved and without an income, it was all but done that she had to move back with her mum. Which, technically, would be fine. Her mum was lovely and adored her. But it would also not be fine because the town of Pyrite was an absolute hell hole in Ruby's eyes. It was a place to escape from, not a place to go back to and lick your wounds. Pyrite had bullies and it didn't matter that she was older now, she was sure those types of small country town bullies never really quit their major preoccupation and they sure as heck didn't leave the town they grew up in. Even if Ruby wasn't their major target, she knew she would come around on their rota of bullying at some point. But it wasn't just that. It was a town filled with straight white people with no redeeming features: no beach or lake. Not even a celebrity had once hailed from there. There were no bars, no botanical gardens and no decent coffee. She shuddered as she thought of the one deli café in the main street that sold BBQ chickens in a foil-lined bag and hot salted chips and didn't have much else except for a noisy humming drinks fridge. A fridge with nothing more than four flavours of fizzy drink. The top four shelves filled with nothing but the same crimson tins of Coke. Ruby doubted they even invested in air conditioning since she left, let alone a coffee machine and properly roasted coffee beans.

The worst thing about Pyrite though was that it didn't have a book shop. Sure, you can buy books online and there was a small library attached to the school in the next town over. The school library that was her haven as a child had been merged with the neighbouring town's library and the space which once held shelves of wonder and beauty was transformed into more classroom space. Her mum broke the news to her as if it were no big deal, as if she had said that the supermarket now opened later on Thursday evenings. But to Ruby, it was a big deal. It was as if a part of her personal history had been erased without her consent.

Pyrite, therefore, having no cave of a bookstore to experience, to run away from the problems of everything that lay outside the walls of the store, was sacrilege. Anytime Ruby walked into a bookstore, whether it be Grayson's or otherwise, being around those tomes of wisdom, altered her state of consciousness. Not that she ever admitted that to anyone, not even Cooper. Because she knew she would sound much like a lunatic. How could a store filled with inanimate products make her feel like she was floating? Like she was a pulsing, energetic version of herself that stretched throughout all time and space and that there weren't really any boundaries between dimensions? Yeah, that's the kind of information that you keep strictly to yourself, even after a few too many dry Rieslings.

Thankfully, at Grayson's, she'd learnt to temper this state of being a little bit. Enough so that she could work without staring at the dancing patterns on the wall in a daze for hours on end. But it still occasionally hit her anytime she browsed through a book store.

Other than Grayson's, there was still a small one left within her neighbourhood— the only brick and mortar competition that Grayson's had. It was a one-room bookstore, no bigger than her dowdy apartment bedroom and didn't hold a lot of the fancy coffee table books— which seemed more appealing to Ruby now that she associated Herman the Creep with these— but it had a handful of popular new releases and lots of quaint finds. Titles like *How to Raise Your IQ by Eating* and *The Jewish-Japanese Sex and Cookbook*. Ruby wasn't really sure how the place made any money, especially these days but it seemed to live on.

At least that's a silver lining, she thought to herself. Visiting the small bookstore without any guilt that she worked for the competition was on the cards. She could even see if the owner, who she believed worked there religiously and infamously never hired anyone, would be gracious enough to give her a few shifts. Hopefully, the word didn't spread that she was fired for assault because who knows how that could only hamper her reputation. Ruby laughed at herself thinking she had any kind of reputation at all. In a city like this, she barely even existed. Which was exactly the way she liked it and why she had chosen to come here and get away from Pyrite once and for all.

The promise of a new job or, at the very least, a new bookstore to explore, gave Ruby the permission she needed to fall asleep that night and wake almost slightly refreshed the next day.

Grimacing at her puffy eyes in the shoddy bathroom mirror she vowed that she would spend no more time crying over losing her job and put all her effort into finding new work. She simply had to. There was always the supermarket or bar work if she had no luck at the small bookstore. Not that she had any experience in either and would certainly be rebuffed for a much younger version with experience and training, especially in this economy.

'No, stop it,' she sternly told herself. 'You are going to be positive about this. You have no choice. Well, that's not true. You have a choice. You can go back home to Shitsville and sponge off your mum. That's your choice. Do you want that?' Ruby gagged at the thought and squirted an extra pump of shampoo into her hand, cleaning her hair as if her future finances depended on it.

Walking through the streets of her neighbourhood, Ruby couldn't help but appreciate the Plane Trees lined up and the festoon lights hung sporadically between them. The pavement was clean and sparkling up at her in the sunlight and she found herself engulfed with a weird sense of optimism. But she was quick to quash it given that her circumstances, on paper, were pretty dire.

Whilst she was listening to her shoes slap on the pavement, Cooper called, the chipper ringtone cutting through her trance and causing her stomach to knot up with anxiety. Reluctantly, she answered fearing his reaction.

'Ruby.' There was no accusation in his tone, only flatness.

Ruby launched straight into defence mode. 'You don't understand, he was going to do something really bad to me.'

'Hey, hey, I get it. I feel for you, buddy. You

shouldn't have been fired. Murray is a total dickhead. Meet me for a drink? Murray is going to close the store today so I get off in a few hours.'

'I'd love to. I really need it,' Ruby exhaled.

'Meet me at Cynthia's in two hours then. I've got an idea.'

'Deal.'

Cooper rang off and she forgot to ask what his idea was. But she desperately hoped he had some kind of plan to help her get her job back. Moreso, she hoped that it didn't involve begging for it or having to deal with Herman ever again.

Ruby sat, or rather slumped, at the bar at Cynthia's, her bag keeping Cooper's seat warm while she waited for him, sipping slowly on cheap wine. Going to the tiny bookstore was nowhere near as fruitful as she had planned and the sense of dread was returning and filling her up once again. The owner looked at her strangely through his thin greasy hair when she enquired about a job and he bluntly told her that there was no work there. In fact, he was thinking about selling the place in a few months as he wanted to move back to England and to not get her hopes up that the bookstore would even be around by year's end. Talk about double heartache.

Ruby felt a hand drag across her back and knew it was Cooper before she even spotted him. His presence usually preceded him. He smiled at her as he plucked her handbag off the stool and slid onto it, without so much as a slight bit of air whooshing up from where his backside hit the seat.

Without talking to her, he requested a bottle of mid-range wine from the bartender and mimed that Ruby drink the dregs of her awful wine. 'What happened?' He inquired gently, without probing.

Ruby relayed the story as he sat appropriately quiet and furrowed his brow at all the right moments. He looked genuinely sympathetic and Ruby was grateful for him and his reaction. A part of her had wondered if he, too, would blame her for getting fired. He already made it clear that he thought she acted the victim when it came to her mounting bills and lack of cash. How would this be any different?

'That's terrible, Ruby. Everything about it is shit. Do you want me to talk some sense into Murray?' He offered kindly.

'No, you need to keep your job and do not need to get into the middle of this. This mess is my own.'

'Good because I already tried to talk sense into him and he did not budge one bit. That arsehole.'

'Oh geez, what am I going to do?' Ruby flung her head down onto her arms dramatically.

'Well, I do have an idea.'

Ruby shot upright. 'Oh?'

'This is a little... strange. A little unorthodox but bear with me.'

'Okay, I'm pretty much down to try anything.' Ruby took a big sip of wine. 'Wait! Not anything. I absolutely will not do any of that multi-level marketing shit.'

Cooper laughed his echoing laugh. 'It's not that. Who do you think I am?' He feigned offence.

As he rummaged in his satchel he said, 'this book came in to work today and I thought you could read it.'

'I certainly have a lot of time to read now that I'm unemployed. Is it *Think and Grow Rich*? Because I'm not sure I can afford to sit around thinking about getting rich without actually getting a job.'

'No, it's not that. Come on now, play nice.'

He pulled a thin book out of his bag and laid it between them. Ruby read the title and scrunched up her face: *Working From Home as Psychic*.

'What the heck?' Ruby stared at the book a little, waiting for Cooper to explain her confusion away.

'I know, I know. It seems a little unorthodox but psychics charge a heap and you could be based at home and work as much or as little as you want. There's potential to earn a lot more than you would have at the bookstore.' Cooper was almost bouncing on the spot, such was his excitement at the proposal. Ruby had never seen Cooper get excited about much. Anything, to be precise.

'Um. I don't really know what to say except these following important things...' Ruby brandished her hand from her lap to begin pointedly counting on her fingers. 'One... no one would come to my daggy arse apartment and sit around my dirty knickers to hear how they are going to strike it rich or find the love of their life. Two... how would I even get clients? I have no money to start advertising for this or know anything about the industry. And three... listen closely fella because this is the real kicker: I'm not psychic! So there goes that idea. What else have ya got?' Ruby threw her hands up in the air.

'Don't just dismiss it, Ruby. You could totally make this work. And, honestly, do you think you really have to be psychic for this job? This is one of the few jobs where you can legitimately fake it and who would even know? All you have to do is tell people that you see them going on a trip in the near future and that they will find love. Tell people what they want to hear and you'll make bank.'

As she let dread and hopelessness overcome her, she watched the bartender wipe up spill after spill and bend down to the fridge to pluck bottles of wine and pour into glasses that needed to be endlessly washed. It looked like a miserable job that Ruby was under-equipped for. She did admire how the woman— a young woman with an impossible tan and even more impossibly bleached hair which was held tightly on top of her head in a ponytail— bent down without so much as a groan or a creak in her knees. Her accent was a distinctly outback Aussie twang and it threw Ruby every time she spoke. It was almost as if Ruby expected her to gallop out of the bar and high jump into the tray of her ute or something.

'I don't really have many other options, do I?'

'Not as I see it. You could at least try this for a little while until you get an interview with a call centre or something. I've heard it takes about a month from registering to even get a phone interview with those places these days. Even the big places like the telcos.'

'Fine.' Ruby swiped the book and slid it into her handbag. 'I'm going to need business cards, an occult looking table cloth and some kind of crystal ball.'

'Let's just start with the business cards.' Cooper took a drink and looked mildly pleased with himself and Ruby didn't know why but it felt good to get his approval and help.

Chapter 3

Chapter 3

After contacting what seemed like three hundred businesses and employment agencies that were advertising for an array of jobs, Ruby's fingers were sore. With each email or online application sent, she could feel the disappointment gather. Most businesses were kind enough to straight-up let her know that her application wouldn't be proceeding thanks to her lack of experience. And with each automatic and carefully worded rejection, a mounting hopelessness beleaguered her.

As the day turned into evening, Ruby was mentally planning the phone call to her mum to request her old bedroom be made up fresh. 'Mum,' she would say, 'move the elliptical machine into the garage, I need my bedroom.'

Just as she was about to log off her computer for the night and wondering how long it would be until she had to sell it, she refreshed her inbox one last time. A request for an interview, at last! Scanning the email with tired eyes, she read that the interview was for the role of receptionist for a large, and impressive, technology company. Well, at least she assumed Crichton Enterprises was a tech company. It was hard to tell from their website as it was riddled with jargon and stock footage of smiling faces that gave nothing away. Nonetheless, her prospects were looking up and her luck had suddenly changed. Even if she did have to stretch the truth in her application about being proficient with phone work. It wasn't a complete lie, she reasoned with herself. She did have to answer the phone at the bookstore when it occasionally rang. Although she didn't really see herself as a corporate receptionist, she was much happier amongst the pages of books, she was fast running out of options and after a day of complete dejection a small twinkle of hope lit her up.

To better her chances, she got ready early the next morning, eagerly practising her answers as she searched around the bottom of her wardrobe for some plain wedge heels that were the closest to corporate attire that she could find. Thankfully, she had a fitted black dress on hand that she used as a standby for funerals, weddings and the like.

Arriving at the ominous building, she felt completely invisible in her outfit that was so intentionally safe that she didn't even notice her own reflection in the mirrored windows. The building loomed higher than any building that she had been in. The outside of the building alone was incredibly intimidating. The oversized automatic sliding doors made the place look like a giant that was swallowing people whole as they entered. Upon a second glance into the reflection of the windows and upon seeing the frenzied people making their way in and out of the building, Ruby knew she didn't belong. Their shoulders were too boxy and sharp, whereas hers were round. Their hands were taken care of and elegant, whereas hers were unattended to and flipped about her side like dying fish.

Turning to look back where she came from, she contemplated skipping across the busy road and falling in a heap on the verge that lined the front of the city's museum. She could already taste the bitterness of the coffee that she would buy and nurse for an hour, maybe more, as she wriggled her backside on the grass and pondered how she could get herself out of the mess that life had thrown at her.

But as she balanced on the gutter, she heard Cooper's accusation come to her. This was one of the moments that he was talking about. Where she chose to be a victim instead of taking control and taking responsibility.

There is absolutely no way you can lose out of this. There's not much that can go wrong here. The worst that can happen is that you don't get a job. You are already unemployed and can't sink much lower! Ruby thought to herself sternly. She sharply turned around and tracked directly into the building, without looking at another.

Thankfully, she was in the elevator alone as her heart was hammering so fast and she was embarrassed to think that someone might hear it. Checking herself in the elevator mirror for one final glance, she swiped her finger underneath her eyes to collect the residue eyeliner that was already melting off. In the morning she decided it was a great idea to go heavy-handed with the eye makeup but now, in the world of busy and important people who spent most of their lives in skyscrapers, she realised she just looked a little ridiculous. Like a cabaret performer that didn't have time to take off last night's make up.

Bracing herself for a stuffy reception office, she waltzed through the open elevator doors and presented herself at the reception desk. Which was, of course, unattended. So she waited. There were no chairs to sit on and she couldn't see anyone either side of the reception area. So she waited some more, awkwardly standing and shifting her weight from one for to the other, hoping someone would pop out eventually. But when no one came after what seemed like at least half an hour to Ruby's urgently beating heart, she decided to make herself known. She certainly wasn't going to leave after she had talked herself into coming this far. And it wasn't like she had anywhere to go or be.

Ruby peered over the spotless desk but couldn't spot a bell to ring or an intercom system. There wasn't even a phone on the desk. Just a notepad and a pen. She felt mighty flustered, her upper arm flesh stuck against her torso as sweat formed. She lifted her elbows out to her sides and flapped them as if she were imitating a chicken, a few times. She gave each underarm a little blow of air.

Perhaps this is a test? She thought. *A way to show initiative by making yourself at home. Maybe, with the employment market so competitive, this is what you have to do to prove yourself these days?* It made total sense to her, so she spied an ajar door to the side of the reception desk and tentatively hovered near it. Poking one eye through the crack, she tried to peer in.

'Yes?' Came a gruff voice from within.

Ruby froze and didn't know what to answer.

'Yes?' This time, a handsome man not much older than her, in a slate grey suit pulled back the door to reveal the shiniest boardroom table Ruby had ever seen. On one side sat a stern and poised looking woman and on the other sat a nervous young woman in a suit.

'I'm... here for the interview?' Ruby posed it as a query mainly because she was questioning herself whether she had dreamt the interview request.

'Wait out there. We'll be with you in a moment.' The man raised his perfectly manicured eyebrows. Ruby had never seen such fine forehead accessories. His face shone a little in the office light, so much so that the tiny bit of stubble poking through could have been mistaken for glitter.

Ruby went to retreat backwards into the reception area but became slightly mesmerised by the man's demeanour and glittery chin. The heel of one of her shoes caught on something underfoot and she slipped backwards. In an instinctual effort to stop herself from landing flat on her back, she half twisted inelegantly and planted her hands and torso on the ground, her legs cartwheeling in the air. One of her shoes flew straight past her head to hit the wall behind her and her handbag skittered across the ground.

Pressing her mouth into the ground, she breathed in the scratchy carpet to stop herself from swearing in humiliation and wondered how she could speedily exit without having to look anyone in the eye. She pulled her knees up a little and pushed back onto all fours and took a deep breath.

'Just thought I'd get in some yoga before my interview,' she tried. But no one laughed. Instead, the handsome man in the grey suit was by her side, also on his hands and knees. Ruby was mystified but remained still, unsure what to do to mitigate embarrassing herself further. The heady mossy scent that he was wearing drifted around her.

'My goodness, are you okay? Please let me help you up.' The man went to awkwardly reach his arms up to lever her up but thought the better of it, wondering how to help her up without inappropriate touch.

'It's okay, I'm totally fine, really.' Ruby

jumped up to standing. 'See, I'm up.' And then instinctively put her hand to her head as she suffered from some light-headedness at getting up too quickly. And maybe it was the trick of the light or, more accurately, the trick of the dizziness but Ruby was really taken by the concern that was webbed across the man's face.

'I'm fine,' she repeated. He scooped down to collect her handbag and the few items that had tumbled out of it. Her keys jangled in his hand as he poured them into her palm but his eyes lingered on the other item he had collected off the floor. It was the book that Cooper had given her.

'Well, that's embarrassing,' she said reaching for the book. 'I'd rather it was a tampon or something.' And then visibly cringed at herself.

'Here's your... book,' the man said.

'Look, I'm just going to go. I suspect I'm a little too uncouth to work here. I want to thank you for the opportunity anyway,' Ruby's mouth was already watering at the thought of a consolatory tangy wine and moan to Cooper that she would arrange the second she was in the lift. If he wanted to label her a victim, then so be it.

'Wait. Stay for the interview at least?' The man wasn't pleading, he said it as if it was simply a fact. And Ruby felt compelled enough by the words to follow where his arm was pointing towards the boardroom where he had come from. Ruby was too discombobulated to even remember to collect her shoe which was flung somewhere and hobbled after the grey suit where he ushered her to sit down. The nervous girl was nowhere to be seen now.

The straightfaced lady across the table stood up and Ruby was overwhelmed by a wall of eggplant suit and a buttercream coloured blouse. Her hand shot towards Ruby. 'I'm Sally, I'm the General Manager and this, who you've met, is Walker. He's our CEO.'

Ruby smiled tightly and a fresh wave of heat rose up through her as she realised she had embarrassed herself in front of the CEO of the company. There was absolutely no way she was getting this job. Mentally, she started preparing where she would store all her books in her mum's house and she imagined them piled up in the bathtub and in kitchen cupboards.

'Look, you're both fancy people in crazy

high-level roles so I am not going to beat a bush fly's tit around with this.' Ruby watched as Sally's head jerked back slightly at her crassness. 'I'm not the best candidate for this job. I've spent most of my time working in a bookstore and I'm not even that great with people.' Ruby shrugged in total freefall now and rubbing her barefoot on the carpet beneath her.

'Life's too short to pretend as you would all know,' she looked them both in the eyes individually as she said this. She was bluffing, basing it on the assumption that everyone wanted to be a little more of themselves and have less of the pretence that society demands. But the way they both squirmed about in their chairs told Ruby more than words could. 'I need a job and I will work hard and diligently and I will fake it as much as you need me to with clients. Or associates. Or whatever comes through this door. Oh, that's another thing. I have absolutely no dicking idea with this place does.' Shrugging her hands up and pressing her lips together so her cheek dimples materialised, Ruby waited for them to explain. But they didn't.

Ruby leant back in her chair and tried to

mentally picture where her shoe fell off, ready to make a quick dash if they were to start lambasting her. A part of her was looking forward to being yelled at, if she was being honest. Her subconscious was begging for a bit of telling off, a reason to fall in a heap and become a victim and feel sorry for herself because her life just wasn't going the way she had planned. By now, at 32, she should be married to a handsome guy, like Walker, and be debating with him about having a second child or whether she should return to the interior design firm she half-heartedly ran. Instead, she was broke, definitely single, unemployed and about to be yelled out by two suits.

But the telling off didn't come. All that came was silence. Capped off by a little more silence. So Ruby pushed herself off the chair, ready to leave.

'Wait, Miss...?'

'Ruby is fine.'

'Ruby. I'd love to talk to you about another opportunity. The reception job... well,' he laughed to himself, 'you're definitely no match for that role. But I have an idea.'

'Why do people keep having ideas around me lately?' Ruby asked no one in particular.

'It's probably something to do with what was in your bag?'

'The small bottle of vodka? Look, I know that looks dodgy but I promise you that I keep that in my bag for hand sanitiser or in case I cut myself and need to treat the wound. And, yes, there was a time when I added it to my hot chocolate one afternoon... I mean evening... when I was in Starbucks. But that was because I was sad and stressed and it was definitely only the once.'

'What you do on your own time is none of my business. But Ruby, you're a psychic obviously. And refreshingly honest. This is outrageous I realise, even in an industry such as ours, but would you consider consulting as the company psychic?'

Ruby chortled. The man had a great sense of humour. But when she met his eyes, she could tell he was being deadset serious.

'Oh! You're serious.'

'I know, you probably make enough money as a private psychic but we could compensate you fairly and you would be free to carry on your psychic business on the side as much as you want.'

Ruby chanced a glance at Sally who had turned the same colour as her eggplant suit and was staring intently at Walker, not bothering to make her disapproval subtle for Ruby's sake.

'Uhh... How would that work exactly?'

'We often need to get the jump on new products or getting a feel for the right in-vestors. Having someone on board to help steer us in the right direction with these things would, literally, be magic.'

'Walker... that's...' Sally trailed off letting her hands show her exasperation.

'Come on Sally, how many times have you said that you wished you could tell the future and how successful we'd be if he had a crystal ball.'

'Yes but hiring some... body... off the street to tell us what we should do with millions of dollars of investments is just...' Sally turned slightly to stare out the window. Her colour had drained and she looked like a deflated balloon. Like someone had finally popped her tight skin so the air could be free of its own accord. '... absurd'. Sally finished her sentence after a long stretch of time.

'It's unorthodox but it's another salary that we'll just spend on the research and development team that, frankly, do the same thing as they all do down there. With very little results. Even if Ruby is only right half of the time, she would still be more valuable than the research and development team.' Walker turned back to Ruby and smiled a powerfully bright smile.

'What do you think? You can have your own consulting office? No assistant, though. I'm sorry.'

'No assistant, that's fine... really. And you would pay?'

'Yes, your consulting fee would be the same as the research and development staff and you get paid monthly.'

Ruby, totally forgetting that she was in no way psychic or even knew the correct terminology or instruments, was swooning over the promise of an income. Of which, she had no idea how much it was.

'I foresee that you will hire a brilliant psychic in the near future!' Ruby said comically.

'Jesus.' Sally threw up her hands and walked out of the boardroom.

Walker just winked at Ruby and said 'she'll come around. She'll definitely come around. Can you start tomorrow?'

Yes, Ruby could definitely start tomorrow.

Chapter 4

Chapter 4

'I thought you said this was an emergency?' Cooper dutifully filled her glass from yet another bottle of acrid wine. Ruby kept a mental tally of how many she owed him.

'It completely is an emergency! Obviously.'

'In what way?'

The curved booth they sat in at Cynthia's gave the illusion of privacy and they felt like they were the only ones there. Even though there was a spattering of patrons that all looked the same.

'Well, harking back... I'm not a psychic, remember?' she asserted.

'You cannot deny that there is something kind of like fate in this. I mean, I've never in my life heard of anyone getting asked to be a corporate psychic consultant before.'

'True. I'm more bewildered that they wanted to hire me for any kind of role after the ludicrous exhibition of awkwardness and uncouthness that I displayed, not once, but twice in the space of fifteen minutes. They can't be a very professional firm. Probably make pharmaceuticals from the bones of small children or something.'

'Yes, that's probably it.' Cooper said drily.

'Okay, so we have a bottle of wine to work out exactly how I'm going to pass as a psychic and make this work.'

'Make that a bottle of wine and four shots of Tequila,' Cooper said as the tanned bartender sourly bought over a tray of wobbling shot glasses.

'Ahhh thinking juice.' Ruby slugged one tequila shot back and didn't move a muscle in her face. Cooper at least pretended to grimace and shudder for effect. It was the most animated Ruby had seen him for some time.

'First things first. If I'm not actually the real deal, I'm going to have to present like one. What do I wear?'

'Black.'

'Thanks to my very banal sense of style and personality, I have that covered.'

'A wig.'

'A wig? You hate my hair, don't you? You always have! Why didn't you tell me sooner?' Ruby fingered a section of her auburn hair which hung heavily on her head.

'Shut up. Your hair is great— beautiful— but you're a professional psychic now so you absolutely, positively need a shiny black bob.'

'I see your point. Got any wigs on ya person?'

'Do I look like some kind of wig carrying guy?'

'Yes,' Ruby said with a straight face.

'Well, I'm not but I'm not above ducking over to the props department of my theatre and seeing what I can find.' Cooper dangled a key in front of her that he had plucked from his pocket. 'I've been needing an excuse to rummage around in the costumes by myself for a while. Every theatre geek's dream.'

'You sure are living up to a certain stereotype, aren't you?'

'You're telling me that you wouldn't go nuts in a theatre costume room if you had the opportunity?'

'Look, you go for your life. I'm going to sit here and keep our tequila warm.'

Cooper returned extraordinarily quickly— or maybe the fuzziness of the alcohol was making Ruby confused about time— with a pregnant canvas bag. He flopped into the booth and whacked the bag on the table triumphantly.

'Okay, I found the most perfect wig, that I really hope you'll return back to me once you've finished with it because I love it. And I found this...' With a small handful of shiny hair, he also plucked out of the bag a woven shawl with fringing that swung with every movement.

'Wow, they are disgusting. I love them.' Ruby was getting a little bit excited about her new venture. Sure, the anxiety of having to pose as an entirely fake career artist was mounting, dulled slightly by the tequila and wine but even if she only managed to bluff her way through half a day, she still got to rock up in all black and wear a killer wig. She told herself to think of it like going to a dress-up party or partaking in some community theatre for a bit. Just until she got paid.

'You look like you're counting in your head,' Cooper said to her.

'I am! I'm counting how much I owe you once I get my first paycheque.'

'Lies, you were counting how many more drinks you can have tonight.'

'Busted.'

'Right, one more and then you need to go home and read that book.'

'Compromise? Two more and ta dahh...' Ruby brandished the book from her bag '... and we read the book here. Chapter one: Developing Your Psychic Intuition. Settle in, Coops, we've got a lot to learn.'

Chapter 5

Chapter 5

Ruby's head felt like a fishbowl of warm water. She shook it a little to stop the goldfish from smacking into the sides of the glass. But the movement caused the whole world to spin and she felt hot bile rise all the way from her toes to her eyeballs.

Sneaking open one eye, she saw her outstretched hand in her blurry vision. A huge spider had overtaken her hand, which caused her to jump up with fright. Her whole body shuddered with nausea at the sudden movement. She wondered if she was about to throw up as she looked to the ground where the large spider lay motionless. Which was, in actual fact, her newly acquired black wig.

'Oh,' she said to herself.

'Oh!' She said again in shock. Her new job!

Cooper and Ruby read through the whole psychic book. Which was great. What wasn't great was that they matched a drink for each chapter they managed. Ruby hoped the information was tucked away somewhere in her memory because the current hangover she was experiencing was so powerful it could have easily given her the amnesia of a coma patient.

'Fu-uck,' Ruby said, disgusted at herself as she realised that she was more than two hours late for her first day on the job.

Welp, I'm basically fired so who cares if I'm a fake psychic, she thought, which strangely, helped to ease the tension and she almost felt excited about the job. "Almost" being the operative word since she mainly just felt sick and craving a hot shower.

By the time she had showered and walked to her new office, she felt remarkably better. There was something also about the black tailored dress, elbow-length leather gloves and knee-high boots that put her in a different mood. Capped off with the wig and shawl and some seriously unhinged kohl eyeliner, Ruby actually felt like she was a different person from the miserable penniless woman she was used to being. *I get the appeal of Cooper's theatre group now,* she thought.

As she rounded the block to face her new destiny, she ran through several semi plausible excuses as to why she was late and her stomach tightened. She was certain she could smell something burning.

'Great, now I'm getting a brain tumour,' she held a gloved hand to her throbbing head but moved it to her agape mouth when she saw the building that housed Crichton Enterprises surrounded by swarms of people and three conspicuous fire trucks. Smoke sat heavy in the air although she couldn't really tell where it was coming from. She spotted Walker in the crowd on his phone looking particularly worried and something shot through her— it was almost a pang of concern.

The second that Walker saw her, he

mouthed 'oh thank God,' and rushed towards her. 'What a way to start your first day, huh?'

'This was certainly not what I was expecting,' Ruby replied.

'Even as a psychic? I'm just teasing. You clearly knew something was up if you've only just arrived.'

Ruby fiddled with her shawl, suddenly feeling completely self-conscious in her ridiculous outfit. She kicked herself thinking that the best way she could have stayed for longer in this job was to remain invisible: one of her secret superpowers.

Sally rushed up to them both and even she looked somewhat relieved to see Ruby.

'Ruby, very glad to see you here and not...'

Walker interjected. 'The fire was supposedly in your new office Ruby. Who knows what kind of danger you would have been in if you came earlier.'

Ruby swallowed away some guilt as she took her opportunity. 'Yes, I did actually sense danger this morning and stayed away but thought I should at least come down to see if everyone is alright.'

'Indeed. Everyone is fine. Only your office has worn the most damage. We'll set you up somewhere else, no problems. I'm sorry you had to start like this. But you look... nice. I hope you don't mind me saying.'

Ruby blushed and dabbed at her eyeliner to make sure it wasn't slipping down her face. Could she actually make this thing work? She tested something. She put her hands to her head, closed her eyes and nodded for a bit, putting on a bit of a show for anyone who was watching.

'I'm sensing that everyone is a little rattled right now and that coffee might be in order?'

Walker laughed, looking relieved. 'Yes, you're certainly right about that.' Walker went to walk away but turned and said, 'you know Ruby, I'm really glad we have you on board. We definitely need someone with your skills. Who knows, you might even be able to help us work out who lit the fire!'

'Oh, it was deliberately lit?' Ruby was shocked. And a little scared.

'Apparently but I can't honestly believe that, you know. Surely it was an accident.'

Ruby looked at Walker and was surprised by the innocence and naivety that poured out of him. She might not be psychic but she did recognise a good person when she saw one.

Ruby was set up in the boardroom in a makeshift office for the day until her new office was cleaned and restored. Having never really worked in an office before, she barely minded and was just glad that she could be on her own whilst she tried to figure out what she could actually do. She made a mental note that she would have to bring in some psychic paraphernalia. She also made a mental note that she would have to work out exactly what psychic paraphernalia was.

After she had been sitting around drinking her coffee for an hour or two and badly craving a croissant, Walker delicately rapped on the boardroom door.

'Hi Ruby, how's things going in here?' Ruby noticed that he'd taken off his suit jacket and wore a muted raspberry shirt paired with a mauve tie. He slid into the boardroom with a bit of a bounce and smiled hard at her. His teeth shone when he smiled and his cheeks slid upwards to reveal deep troughs under his eyes. Ruby had a fleeting thought that she really enjoyed when this man smiled and something in her wanted to make sure she caused a smile or two.

'Things are fine. I guess this isn't a typical day on the job with everyone still rattled by the fire.'

'Yes, the smoke smell is still lingering, isn't it? We'll get you set up with the usual HR stuff— like contact and bank account details— today and there are a few things that Sally and I had in mind that we could get your... insights on. Have you met Lucy yet? Lucy is Sally's assistant but much more than that really.'

'No, I haven't met her yet. What's she like? Hopefully not as scary as Sally.' Ruby meant it as a joke but realised in horror at her mistake of letting her mouth run off over what was essentially one of her bosses. For all she knew, Sally and Walker were an item. Although the friction between them suggested otherwise.

Walker caught her eye and smiled that smile again. 'I know what you mean about Sally. She is a great person, once you get to know her. She just presents differently to others. I'll get Lucy.'

'Great, send her in.' Ruby looked up at the vision that had entered the doorway whilst they were chatting. In walked one of the most glorious people that Ruby had ever seen. A five-foot-five man with pointy heeled yellow boots, white tight pants and an oversized cable knit jumper that hung down to his knees. He broadly smiled at her and tapped his fingertips together in front of his face, as if he were pretending to be an evil villain from a movie.

'Darling, Lucy is not a she. It is I. And I, for the most part, identify as male' Lucy swept in towards Ruby and held out a hand smugly.

'Oh my goodness, I'm so sorry for misgendering you.' Ruby was as embarrassed as she was taken by Lucy's presence.

'Truth be told, it happens all the time. But there's no chance in hell, pun intended, that I'm using my full birth name of Lucifer. I mean seriously, what was my adoptive mother thinking? Anyway, welcome to the fray, my little witch. First things first, will the love of my life hurry up and make himself available to me?'

Lucy perched on the edge of the table and cocked an eyebrow and Ruby couldn't tell if he was serious or not. He swept his spectacular shoulder-length hair off one shoulder and let it effortlessly fall back where it was. Ruby could tell that it was all for show and he wanted it made known that he was to be the attractive one around the office. Ruby wanted to assure him that there was absolutely no competition.

Remembering that Walker was still in the room, Lucy gathered himself and hopped off Ruby's workspace and cleared his throat. 'Fine. If you have any questions about this place, I'm happy to help. I've got a bunch of HR files that mum and dad...' Lucy gestured towards Walker, '...want you to go through. Let me just pop on some more eyeliner first— can't have you outdoing me in those stakes can we baby-doll? Hmm?' Lucy walked evenly out the door and Walker followed hurriedly, declaring 'good luck' back at Ruby.

Okay, she would have to fake some things but Walker seemed lovely and Lucy was just the kind of person she would love to spend her days with, so the job could be something that she could utterly get used to. Enjoy even.

Ruby tried to think back to what the psychic book had told her and searched her memory for absolutely any piece of wisdom from it. But nothing came. What's worse is that she couldn't really remember much from the point after when Cooper returned with the wig and shawl. She made a silent little promise to herself to not drink so much again, especially now she had a new job that she desperately needed to keep and get paid for.

Chapter 6

Chapter 6

'Girl, here.' Lucy dumped a bunch of manila files in front of her. He had not only done his eyeliner but applied a plum lip gloss as well, which made his olive skin pop even more.

'You want me to read these? Enter them into the computer? Or...' Ruby frowned and held up a palm.

'Darl, you're not a temp, you're a psychic. Sal wants you to go through each file and tell us what you can about the employee inside. HR has redacted any identifying info— names, job title and so on.'

'What kind of info is she looking for?'

'Basically, whatever you can glean. Think along the lines of doing anything wrong or corrupt against the company or in the process of finding a new job. Or even if they have super potential that we overlook. Which, to be brutally hand to heart, is probably ever mother flippa in this joint, ya know? Everyone potentially gets overlooked and no one gets promoted. For years.' Lucy paused and pursed his lips. 'Or am I projecting?' He laughed it off and tapped his hand on top of the files. 'Anyway, have fun with that, Witchy.'

'Look forward to it.'

'Lunch at the sushi train with me?'

'Would be delighted.'

Ruby ran her finger over line by line of each file but nothing really stood out to her. She couldn't very well go back to Sally and say that she found nothing, could she? Sally didn't want to hire her in the first place so any excuse to shove her out, she'd be looking for. What if this was a test? *I must find something,* Ruby thought to herself. *I have two options: I make some stuff up that is benign enough to be unconfirmed or that the person would not be inclined to admit.*

Or, I study each file hard enough. Even data can reveal truths that people have not been willing to see. You don't have to be psychic when you're working with facts.

Ruby froze as Walker came into the boardroom solemnly. *Uh oh, this is it. This is where I get fired,* thought Ruby. Flipping together the open file in front of her, she shifted it to the side and crossed her legs and clasped her hands at the same time. She was going to beg, she'd decided. Now that they had met her, surely she'd have more of a chance to slide into another role and Walker seemed like a decent enough guy that he wouldn't be able to resist some old fashioned begging.

'Ruby, I need to tell you something. And given that you are a psychic, you have no doubt already picked this up and know this about me. Nonetheless, it's hard to say out loud but I feel that I need to. To clear the air between us and start from a base of truth.'

Ruby felt blindsided. There was this charismatic and in charge man, on the verge of tears and crumpled before her ready to confess something that was obviously colossal. Maybe they didn't really understand what a psychic was and thought that she could double as a counsellor. Thinking of her books in her mother's bathtub, Ruby was so desperate for the money that she would have pretended to be anything at that point in time.

Ruby scrounged. 'Yes, I have picked up some things about you but sometimes it's best that I hear them in your own words.' *Congratulations, Ruby*, she thought to herself. *You're in tits deep now.*

'No one, I think, knows this about me here. And, of course, I would appreciate your utmost confidentiality.'

'Of course. I don't really have anyone to tell anyway. But even if I did, us psychics are bound by an unspoken rule to maintain confidentiality where possible.' *Another bold lie there, Ruby.*

'I have really strong feelings for someone in the office. Of course, being the boss it's completely unethical and illegal for me to approach them and tell them. But I'm almost certain they feel the same way!'

'Oh.' Was all Ruby could muster as she ran through the people that she knew in the office.

It didn't really fit that it was any of them. Sally? It had to be. Cooper's voice rang through Ruby's head. "Just tell people what they want to hear."

'Yes, I knew that from the moment I met you,' Ruby mollified. 'And I'm getting a strong sense that they, too, feel the same way. But you're right, it could be a disaster, profession- ally speaking, to reveal your true intentions.'

'I thought so! I was right. You're so bang on.' Walker looked relieved as he looked at the win- dow. 'But what am I to do?' The pain in his voice overtook him as he threw his head in his hands and started sobbing so loudly that she was sure that someone would come in to see if a donkey was mating.

Ruby awoke with a start. One side of her face pressed into a file she was halfway through reading. She realised the loud sobbing she heard and thought was Walker, was actually her own snoring piercing through her dream- scape. Disorientated, Ruby looked around the room. There was no one there— not Walker or anyone. The files were spread out before her awaiting her attention. A wet spot the size of a coin had formed from her drool making the ink bleed. Shaking her head to absolve herself of the dream, she took some deep sharp breaths. It would not do if she was going to fall asleep on the job. She was extraordinarily lucky that no one had caught her.

In perfect timing, Lucy rolled his head around the corner and quipped, 'sushi?'

Admittedly, that the little nap had shaken off the last of her hangover headache and she was dying for some sushi.

As she sat next to Lucy watching the sushi train roll around as slow as her mind felt and listening to him talk about how dramatic is on-line fantasy football league was getting, Ruby couldn't stop thinking about the dream she had about Walker. It wasn't like her to dream about people she hardly knew. It must have been the hangover, she thought.

Ruby kept smiling and nodding as Lucy divulged all about himself as she pretended to sip on the green tea. She actually hated green tea but felt it unbecoming not to pretend, especially when eating sushi.

Lucy abruptly stopped his conversational

train. 'Anyway, enough about my boring life. Let's uncover the Ruby story. Single?'

Ruby hesitated. 'Madly.'

'We'll have to fix that then. Grew up in the city?'

'Unfortunately, not. Grew up in Pyrite and hate it. It's kind of my hell on earth, if you know what I mean?'

'Do I ever. Small towns are hellscapes for people like you and me. We're too big for them.'

'Thankfully, I have a shitty apartment in that red building around the corner from Cynthia's Bar and I can now walk to work.'

Ruby already felt too exposed and like she had let too much information slip out of her. If she wasn't careful, she would end up revealing herself as a charlatan to Lucy within the first week. She artfully directed the conversation back to him.

'And what about your love life? More importantly, where did you get those amazing shoes?'

Ruby had said the right thing. Lucy glowed at the compliment and held one foot up, flexing it up and down from the ankle.

'I have a lovely friend down in the village

who makes bespoke shoes for iconic peeps like me. Shoes are my thing. Well, really a lot of things are my thing but shiny, bold shoes are up there. I'll take you to him one time. He's a quaint old bugger, our Edwardo. His husband died of cancer a few years ago and he hasn't really got over it. Maybe you could talk to his dead husband for him?' Lucy arched an eyebrow and Ruby couldn't help but feel like it was an accusation. Did Lucy already see through her pathetic charade? Perhaps Sally had convinced him to find out that she was a fake.

'I don't typically do medium work.' *Good girl Ruby, keep it up.* 'And I promised myself that I would focus all my psychic energies on this job with Crichton. It can be exceptionally draining, you know.' Ruby engaged her new signature move of putting her hand to her head to indicate there was something happening around her in the supernatural realms.

Tucking away in her mind, she told herself that she would have to find a way to convince Lucy that she was a psychic. Having him on her side could be the way to win Sally's approval. Ruby had watched how they fake flirted with each other and how much Sally respected his opinion. Just before they went to lunch, Sally popped over to Lucy's desk and asked 'I just want to check, hair up or down for this thing I have to go to on the weekend?' Without looking up, Lucy rattled back 'down, with that side clip with the pearls.' Ruby smiled at his astuteness.

'Oh and the little round earrings, not the square ones,' he shouted back to Sally as he grabbed Ruby by the hand and pressed the button for the elevator.

Looking at her untouched tuna rolls which she drowned in soy sauce, Ruby declared 'hey, let's do you a love reading sometime soon. I'm already getting a sense there's someone around you that has their eye on you!' It wasn't such a psychic stretch for Ruby as Lucy was a gorgeous and social guy and there was bound to be at least half a dozen potential suitors floating around his magnetic orbit.

'Oohh you are good, Witchy. There's this guy... let's call him Jesus. That's not his name, it's just that he's a carpenter and you know the fable. Personally, I don't because I've never read *The Bible* in my gosh darn life but we can all agree that our man Jesus was a carpenter. Anyway, I met carpenter at Juicy's which is this terribly tacky gay bar— we absolutely must go sometime— and I don't know... he seems to be playing kind of coy. Which, if you ask me, is a gosh darn waste of time in this day and age. Especially as I near thirty, I am not getting any younger. But I am getting hotter... so there is that.' Lucy waved to a trio of twinks that had just walked in, who clearly knew him.

Ruby nodded enthusiastically, remembering every bit of information that she could as she didn't know exactly when it would come in handy. She would have to start writing stuff down. It's a lot to remember when you're playing psychic.

Turning away from the twinks he said, 'Anyway, let's hustle back. Sal gets a bit crotchety if I don't get back in time.'

Ruby happily followed him back to the office, which still smelt mildly of smoke, she noticed.

Chapter 7

Chapter 7

At the end of the day, Ruby grinned the whole way home walking through some of her favourite streets of the city. As she sauntered past the shop windows, all lined up pressed together boasting their wares, she realised she made it through the first day without too many hiccups. Especially if you didn't count a building fire, falling asleep at her desk and misgendering her colleague as hiccups. But importantly, she'd gotten away with basically having no skills whatsoever except telling people what they want to hear. If this is what it took to make a living, she would be totally, one hundred per cent on board with that.

As she climbed up the cement stairwell in her drab apartment building, she listened to the heavy echo of her high heeled boots as she took each step. The thrumming had replaced her hangover headache and she was excited to see what outfit she would scrummage together for her next day of work. There was a cape that was sitting at the back of her wardrobe that was just begging to be used. Maybe even a touch of purple eyeshadow if she felt bold.

The rickety door opened unusually easily for her and breathing the biggest sigh of relief she had in her, she stepped over a threshold that was clean of demanding and intimidating letters for once. But she knew it wouldn't be this way every night, the stressful letters would start coming again soon. And just because she threw them unopened in the bin, didn't mean that the problems disappeared. Ruby imagined the sensation in her body of never having to cower just coming home to her own place to find worrying letters strewn about the place. Or constant phone calls, reminder texts and emails from utility companies about her over-due bills. It seemed impossible. But if she grasped, her imagination could find it. *If I can imagine it, it surely must be achievable?* Many widely shared success quotes boasted something of the sort.

Grateful for the small reprieve of a letterless floor, she scurried through her apartment eager to hang her outfit out ready for the next day. There was no way she was going to be late a second time.

The outfit she chose: the knee-length poncho cape and skinny dark grey jeans, coupled with a chunky heel, really delighted her. So she carefully undid her wig and shimmied out of the clothes and placed them on a chair near her bed.

Looking around the room for the final touch, she went in search of her black nail polish which had been left untouched since the previous Halloween. But she noticed something, something that wasn't supposed to be there.

Next to her bed, the bedside table had been knocked a few inches askew. And the psychic book was strewn on the other side of the bed-side table. Looking up at her forlornly like a lame bat.

And then Ruby remembered, she had been so wasted the night before that she was surprised she didn't sleep on the bathroom floor. A place she had frequented after nights out in her early twenties. Something about the cool, sleek tiles was incredibly appealing and she thought about having a quick lay down now against them. Stealing a glance towards her glossy white bathroom floor tiles she watched as they changed in the light. There was no doubt in Ruby's mind that she'd just seen a shadow swipe past on them. The bathroom window and blind were closed though.

Every hair on her body stood on end and her mouth salivated out of dread. *Boy, this hangover is really getting to me*, she thought. *It's just simple, old fashioned paranoia. Have a glass of water and a lie-down, you silly old chook.*

But just to be sure, Ruby looked for where she had ditched handbag, which held her phone, upon arrival. She leapt towards it, which lay like a deflated blob on her bed. Before she could reach it, however, she felt a warm sting in the back of her head and watched her bedroom turn sideways on her. One side of her entire body: from her shoulder, down her arm, her thigh and even her foot, crashed in pain to the floor. The throbbing beginning the moment of impact. Her eyesight went completely black before she even knew what was happening.

Chapter 8

Chapter 8

On the other side of her closed eyes, Ruby could sense bright light and a cacophony of bird sounds swam around her thick head.

Well, it must be morning, she thought to herself. *I better get up and get ready for...* Reluctantly, she peeled her eyes apart. Simultaneously, she lifted her torso and remembered what happened the night before. The back of her head felt like it had been crushed. The pain radiated across her scalp and down her jaw. A quick scan down her body revealed she was still in her underwear from the day before. And the thick streak of black across one eye told her that, although askew, she had slept in her wig. Thankfully nothing had been removed. Gingerly, she lifted a hand to her face and stroked it. It was a little bit tense from sleeping on the floor but there weren't any traces of blood.

'Get up,' she heard a voice. Shit, there was still someone in her house. She froze, shut her eyes and lay back down again. Terrified, she held her breath as if that would do anything to protect her. *Let them rob the place blind, there's basically nothing here for them of value*, she reasoned with herself.

'Darling, get up,' the melodic voice sung out again.

Quite sweet robbers, if you ask me, Ruby thought. *But I'm not getting up so they can terrorise me. I'll just lay here until one of us gets bored and I once did not move from my bed for three days straight reading the entirety of the VC Andrews Dollanganger series. I have it in me you jerks.*

'You need to go to work. Get up.' Ruby couldn't ignore the angelic voice and tentatively looked around her bedroom but had no desire to get up. Especially, if she had been burgled and the place was trashed. Although small, cleaning her apartment of mess and chaos would be exhausting and time-sucking.

But upon scanning the room, she realised that nothing had really changed in there. Even her handbag remained on the bed, awaiting her. It seemed to be saying to her that it couldn't wait to go to work again. And despite the pain that radiated from the back of her head, Ruby felt a little the same. At least she might feel a little safer than in her apartment.

'Who's here?' Ruby shouted shrilly. *Ugh*, she thought. *Is that the right thing to say to someone or some people who have broken into your house, who are probably keen on a bit of sexual assault if they didn't find anything of worth.*

Silence greeted her back so she cleared her throat and tried again. 'My boyfriend's a cop.' *Big deal*, Ruby, *she thought to herself.* How will that scare them if the damage is already done? Besides, anyone could tell by the fraught tone in her voice that she was lying.

Her back was starting to ache from being on the dusty floorboards and she was sick of looking at the patterns on her doona cover. She really just wanted the hottest coffee she could make and to get to work.

A boldness came over her. 'Alright, get the flip outta my house now if you're still here. I've gotta go to work.' *Criminals are notoriously known for listening to the logical pleas of a pathetic woman in her early thirties*, she thought sarcastically.

But there were no sounds and no movement and when Ruby garnered enough bravery to poke her head into the kitchen-cum-lounge room and sweep her eyes around the entire dingy apartment, she realised she was alone. They— whoever had been here and knocked her out— even had the decency to shut the front door behind them.

Ruby was jumpy as she showered and dressed. With every small movement she made, she looked around to double-check that she was alone. She put on her underwear and then leant her torso through the bedroom door to see if she was still alone. And then she put on her skirt and would repeat the pattern. Quickly reaffixing her wig, she made sure her eyes or ears weren't covered longer than a split second so she could be on alert.

The strange thing was that she noticed they hadn't stolen anything— *suckers,* she thought— and wondered if it was even worth going to the police. What if they did a blood alcohol reading on her and it was still foolishly high from two nights ago and they pegged her as some lonely alco that tripped over her own untidiness. Surely, she didn't trip, did she? There had to have been someone in her place. The tender spot at the back of the head that cried out as she adjusted her wig proved it.

Thankfully, she didn't have much time to dwell on it at Crichton Enterprises as Sally was up her arse about the wretched HR files task. 'Oh yes,' Ruby promised. 'I unearthed a few things, I'll put together some kind of report for you...' she trailed off as she walked past her pretending to be busy.

'Very well,' Sally resigned.

A little while later, Ruby had all but forget about the intruder and her sore head. Happily, she was stationed in the boardroom and already felt like part of the team in her new workplace.

Lucy had brought in a takeaway coffee for her first thing, with nothing but a wink and a smile. Ruby was eternally grateful to have a work buddy.

Walker stormed in as she was poring over a rather tedious file and wondering if she could jeopardise the poor person's career by pretending she had visions of them interviewing with a competitor.

'Ruby, I have a very important task for you and I just know you're up to the job. Swing by my office in twenty, if you would be so kind.' Walker's jubilance was attractive and effective. Despite herself, Ruby found herself enthusiastic because of it.

Barely waiting fifteen minutes, mainly so she didn't have to keep staring at the boring file of Employee X who had worked at Crichton Enterprises for six years now and had no outstanding commentary about their entire time there. She pinched up the ends of the poncho cape and walked into Walker's office.

'How very *Downtown Abbey* of you Miss Ruby,' Walker laughed upon seeing her waltz in.

Ruby blushed and dropped the cape, embarrassed at her failed attempt at having some decorum. *Why start now?* she thought to herself.

Suddenly, Ruby's vision blurred around the edges and she was sure a migraine or fainting spell was about to become her. *Those absolute turds*, she thought. *Surely, they didn't have to bang me on the head and ruin my chances of keeping a job. If I have brain damage, I will sue someone. Not sure who but...*

A whooshing sound, like a bullet train sucking past her, roared in her ears and she had to breathe deeply to retain her balance. It all but split her head in two. She tried hard to focus on Walker in front of her as her field of vision became fuzzy. It was as if she was looking at everything through a lace doily. His words faded into the background and the whooshing noise obliterated everything that came out of his mouth. Where his chest was, a large red heart burst through. It looked like a cartoon heart from the Disney VHS tapes she used to watch as a kid, before she discovered books. The love heart was juicy and dripped with globules of blood. The source of the blood was the glaring wound that protruded right through the centre of the heart, caused by a burnished sword. It reminded Ruby of the Three of Swords tarot card that featured in her psychic book a lot.

'Your heart... it's...' At the sound of her own voice, her vision returned to normal, focussing with clarity again and the heart faded away as if it were never there.

'Yes?' Walker asked concerned.

'Oh, I'm sorry. I thought... I seem to have a headache.' Ruby gripped at her head, trying to squeeze the remnants of the vision and the pain away with her hands. The back of her head was pounding, her thoughts all runny and swirly like melted ice cream.

'Did you see something Ruby? Do you have any psychic words of wisdom for us?' Walker asked jovially.

His warmth encouraged Ruby to relax and which meant the disturbing image had all but faded into a distant memory. 'Not quite, please do continue. Sorry to interrupt you.' Ruby returned her full attention to what Walker was saying.

'Right, well be sure to share anything you think might be useful. I'm really quite open to it, as I hope you have gathered. As I was saying, we've pitched our latest round of ClairTech to two potential investors. They are both extremely interested, at least that's what the contact of each organisation has verbally promised. The trouble is, we can only go with one as they are, technically, competitors. And we can't have each company finding out that the other is in the running to be our future investor. We've kind of made a bit of a balls up about it, really. But nonetheless, it's still salvageable.'

Ruby nodded blankly, her mind still tripping back to the weird hallucination she just had. Blows to the head are never a good thing, really. Could she afford to see a doctor about it? Maybe she could get an advance on her pay.

'Anyway, this is where you come in. I'm going to set up a meeting with both companies with you. Separately of course. And if there's anything, anything at all that you see or hear or pick up from the meetings that would lead us in the direction of a positive investment decision, well you would be worth your weight in gold.' Walker swiped a hand through his hair and, to Ruby, it was endearing but it also revealed the kind of stress he was under. It dawned on her that this job wasn't a joke for him like it was for her. This was his company and there were serious things at stake. Lots of money too, she'd imagined. He must have been desperate to go down the route of hiring a stranger who purported to be a psychic.

'Is there one candidate that shines out above the other? Or a preference of who you would like to go with?' Ruby asked earnestly. She found herself actually wanting to help Walker.

'Not really. Both have pros and cons but at the end of the day, we just really need the money to get back up to scratch with all our back catalogue of products and invest in some better research and development. ClairTech has absolutely enormous potential. It's going to be something that revolutionises the world and I don't say that lightly.'

Ruby assumed it was all hyperbole. Any tech CEO would have to believe in their own product like it was their own offspring. 'What kind of product is it?'

Walker looked taken aback and Ruby felt completely foolish. How could she just admit to her boss that she had no idea what her place of employment actually did? Backtracking she said, 'I mean, I know what kind of product it is. I think I meant to say what is it about the product that appeals to the investors?'

Walker faltered, 'There's a lot riding on this, unfortunately. I don't mean to put undue pressure on you. But without a colossal investment, we are just kind of spinning our wheels in the dirt.' Walker sighed and loosened his tie a little. 'I think I can speak candidly with you when I say that without a decent investment sometime soon, we're as good as going bust.'

'I see.' Ruby's stomach started churning. How the crap was she going to pull this off? At least she only had a fifty-fifty chance of getting it wrong.

'And getting it right,' a soft voice came out of nowhere. Ruby furrowed her brow. She must have imagined it. Maybe it was a side effect of concussion when you hear your own thoughts as a disembodied voice. *How fun that will be,* she thought.

She stood up to leave Walker's office but wobbled on her feet a little. Again, Ruby's vision went blurry around the edges and double vision swam in front of her. The noise rushed in but it was less alarming this time, less overwhelming. Instead, it sounded like ocean waves that continuously hitting the shore. Ruby stared hard through the obscure lace and was determined to see what was behind it. With the strong intention, the lacey effect dropped away. Like a magician flicking away a table cloth. On the other side of the lace was the clearest vision, as if it was happening right in front of her in real life. *Damn, hallucinations are getting good these days,* Ruby thought to herself.

Walker reached out a hand towards her, like he was reaching out for someone to save him from drowning. His bulbous fingertips almost reached her and Ruby couldn't tell if he was going to strangle her or needed her help. Deeply etched into his face was signs of misery.

'I love you.' He pleaded desperately. His eyes welled up.

'Excuse me?' Ruby thought she said, stunned.

'I love you. I'm in love with you!' His face crumpled in agony as he continued to reach out an unclasped hand.

Ruby blinked her eyes a few times and pinched her thigh. The ocean noise ceased and she looked back to Walker who was shuffling some papers on his desk happily whistling to himself. The cyan cuffs of his shirt poking out now and then with his movement.

'Sorry, did you say something Ruby? I'll let you know when the meetings have been set up, okay? Should be this week.'

'Sure. That sounds great,' she said cautiously.

Ruby backed away from Walker out the door and bumped straight into Lucy who had been waiting outside Walker's office for her. Ruby shuddered and hoped Lucy had witnessed Ruby's peculiar behaviour if only to solidify her performance of being a psychic.

'Hey, girl, hey.' He said smiling at her and appraising her outfit with a look up and down. Lucy himself had on glossy black boots, skinny jeans and a black turtle neck and one bold yellow plastic stare shaped earring. He looked terrific.

'You look terrific Lucy.'

'Don't I? Lunch again today?'

Ruby nodded appreciatively and a small feeling swam up inside her that felt a little like she was at home in this quaint job in a world that she ordinarily didn't belong. Most of all, she was pleased to have someone like Lucy who she could call her friend.

Chapter 9

The two investor meetings gave her nothing. Not even a hint of anything. The first was a bland middle-aged man in a just as bland suit. He was so bland, that she was sure he introduced himself as Blandy instead of Andy at one point. The second meeting was almost quite as dull. The man, this time his name didn't even stick, was sweating and red-faced and had the demeanour of a horny bulldog but nothing struck out to Ruby as to which way the company should swing. Which, in a way, gave her great comfort because she was sure there was no wrong answer.

That was until she was sitting still in the boardroom after the second meeting, wondering which of the two bland men she will recommend to Walker when she heard the soft voice out of nowhere again.

'Neither are suitable investors.' Ruby froze. Surely, that was not her own thoughts. Particularly as it would make her life much more difficult if she were to present that to Sally and Walker. Sally had barely acknowledged her in the week that she had been there except to push her face into Ruby's and say 'any idea which investor yet?' and then pursed her lips when Ruby said she was close but just wanted to make absolutely sure since a lot was riding on the recommendation.

Ruby waited and asked the air. 'Which investor?'

'Neither investor.' There it was. Completely unmistakeable. A voice. It sounded so close to her ear too. It was a lovely voice. A comforting, almost angelic, female voice.

'Are you an angel?' she asked it. To which she received no reply.

'Neither investor.' The voice was more forceful this time. She couldn't possibly go to Walker and say that they need to start the investor scouring process all over again, surely?

Ruby touched the back of her head, her fingers searching underneath the wig for a bump but came up empty except for a small twinge of bruise-like pain that was still there.

Perplexed, Ruby walked out the building to get some fresh air. There's no way that sitting inside an office all day, still with the residue of smoke could be good for the brain. It was clearly affecting her. It smelt like melted plastic.

Sitting at the base of a metal pyramid sculpture that someone had obviously thought looked great at one point in time, she let the sunlight dance across her jeaned legs and instantly felt better. *Fresh air and sunlight, that's all I needed. There's nothing wrong with me. I'm not going crazy or have a concussion, I'm just getting used to the corporate life. No big deal,* she thought. As she consoled herself with that realisation, an electric pulse shot up her arm. Her arm felt freezing cold yet on fire at the same time. Looking down, she expected to see tiny metal spikes pierce up through her skin but instead, she saw a hand with scallop-shaped nails.

'Sorry Ruby, I didn't mean to startle you. I just saw you sitting here and wanted to check how you are going?' It was Walker. His handsome face beaming back down on her with the same concern that must have been his default position. Ruby guessed that someone who was under constant stress and worry would be the first person to spot the symptoms in another.

'Totally fine, thanks, Walker. Just catching a breath o' fresh, ya know?'

'Indeed. Mind if I sit?' Still impeccably polite.

A part of Ruby wanted to say "yes, leave me alone for five so I can figure out just how insane I'm going" but her mouth was still too much of a people pleaser to obey. 'By all means.'

Walker sat gracefully next to her and she could occasionally feel the fabric of his suit sleeve brush against her own try-hard ensemble. A growing discomfort arose in her as they sat awkward and silent next to one another. Walker had a crush on her. Or was falling in love with her, according to her strange apparitions. Which, of course, they surely couldn't be. *Do concussions cause delusions?* she wondered. *They must, surely. It's part of the hallucination family, no doubt.*

Now, this placed Ruby in a white-hot dilemma. Walker was incredibly handsome and, most likely, loaded. He was intelligent as heck and he was surely a good person. The amount of time he spent checking to see how Ruby was doing when she was nothing but a lowly employee, spoke volumes. And he smelt... like Christmas trees.

Stop it. Stop it, Ruby told herself. She absolutely could not have herself developing a crush on her boss who she hardly knew. But her fantasy had already started to unfurl and was already galloping out of her control. If she were to start dating Walker— *gosh, where would their first date be? A bar? A helicopter ride out to a nearby vineyard?—* then she would surely have to give up her job. Thinking back to her contract and the remuneration that was highlighted at the top was a surefire anchor to her keeping the job. *Okay, but what about...* she questioned herself, *...if I became Walker's trophy wife? Surely, he'd earn enough for both of us. I might be bored as shit but I could soon find hobbies to occupy my days. I could learn to cook! And make him dinners! I suppose I could join Cooper's daggy theatre group. Which reminds me... his performance is coming up soon. I must check my phone when that is. Can't wait for that to suck away three hours of my life.*

'Sorry, did you say something?' Walker quizzed.

'Oh, just... talking to the...' Ruby circled her hand around in the air hoping she was still pulling off being a psychic.

'Ahh, I see. You know, my aunt was a psychic. A medium, I think. They the ones that talk to dead people?'

'Yeah,' Ruby seemed to recall the book saying something along those lines.

'Anyway, one day...'

Ruby had to cut Walker off. She clasped his forearm with the grip of a gorilla as the area around him as well as the front of the building started to wobble and vibrate. Walker faded from view as if being sucked back into a tunnel and all Ruby could see were stripes of light and yet she could still feel the ground shaking. And a strong hand on her back.

Another vision was happening and Ruby had no prepared herself. Again, Walker said in all earnest, 'I love you. I love you,' His face pushed together as he said the word 'you' and Ruby could tell the urgency behind his words.

'Me?' Ruby found herself asking the vision. But the apparition version of Walker didn't answer her. It just kept repeating the words. The more Ruby stared at this form, the more it faded and was replaced with shiny blackness. Like a reflective black pond to be found at the bottom of a garden surrounding a haunted manor. It gave her the chills but something inside of her felt compelled to keep looking. There had to be something within that blackness. A message, a vision or something. Ruby waited and strained her eyes at the whim of the murk as it reflected nothing but a sheen back to her, its patience endless.

Ruby focussed on the warm imprint of the hand that melted through her top and felt like it seeped through to the centre of her chest and just as quickly as it came on, the vibrating and the blurriness faded away. There was Walker, right in front of her leaning in closer. His lovely forehead dripping down between his eyes with concern.

'Ruby, you okay? You look kind of… peaky.'

'I'm sorry, I just…' Ruby leapt up and tapped the ground with her foot twice to see if it was stable to walk upon. There was no sign of quivering ground so she skittered off, away from Crichton Enterprises and the blurry vision and from Walker. Whose warm handprint she could still feel lingering on her.

Chapter 10

Chapter 10

Thankfully, the city hospital was not too far away and the short walk made Ruby's senses come around a lot more. She was mentally kicking herself. *What fool doesn't go straight to the hospital after they have been whacked in the head? Here I am having been suffering from a pretty bad concussion for days. Shit, my brain is probably a big bowl of blood soup up there in my noggin.*

Chewing on her lip Ruby contemplated two worrisome things. Firstly, how to explain to a doctor that she'd been seeing tunnel-like visions of blackness and people declaring their love?

And secondly, how exactly was she going to pay for the medical expenses? *It's fine*, she reasoned, *I'll just pay for this out of my first paycheque from Crichton Enterprises and if my phone has to get cut off for a bit, so be it. I can't work and earn more money if I'm in a coma or drowning in my own brain blood, can I?*

In the hospital, Ruby waited an excruciating length of time to be seen to. The waiting room of the A and E department was surprisingly full for a weekday afternoon and there was a cacophony of children crying and hunched over elderly men grumbling at the staff behind the Perspex screen of the admissions desk. Across from her sat a middle-aged man whose oval-shaped belly dared Ruby to stare at it. She could make out the rut of his belly button beneath the fawn-coloured t-shirt which was thin and unclean. Ruby forced herself to peel her eyes off his stomach and look at his face. There was a lot of pain that hung in that man's face and Ruby felt ashamed to gaze directly at it. The lines that shot out from the corners of his eyes told of his personal history and it was riddled with sadness. Truly, Ruby knew that the physical pain he was in, the reason why he was in the waiting room was no match for the emotional torment that life had tortured him with.

In a new way of being to Ruby, she found her eyes welling up and the centre of her chest burning, like it wanted to crack itself open and let a bunch of little lava critters run out into their freedom. Sure, she could smell the unpleasant dusty cheese smell that wafted over from the man. If he had come into the bookstore when she was working there, she would have avoided him at all costs. Perhaps hidden out the back and bribed Cooper with a chocolate ice cream to serve him. But right there, in the waiting room, in the centre of vulnerability, Ruby had nothing but frank heartfelt empathy and it overtook her senses. If her heart could turn itself inside out and swallow her whole body, and his too, it would have at that moment.

To prevent herself from weeping or taking the stranger in her arms, she looked away and forced herself to read the instructional posters

over and over until the words lost their meaning. If she let her eyeline slip and fall to any of
the fellow patients, she experienced a similar
feeling to when she looked at the man. A robust
sensation across her chest and an overwhelming feeling of wanting to cry, to take away every
sting and pain that convalesced in the epicen-
tre of hurt.

The waiting and witnessing of others' pain
wasn't so much the uncomfortable part for her.
It was the fact that the noise and fluorescent
lighting of the place had amplified Ruby's head
injuries so much that her vision alternated between blurry, hyper-focused and wavering, like
the steam off a bitumen road on a hot day. But
even through all that, the tangible empathy still
lingered from the man in front of her. This only
served to convince her more that she needed a
doctor. And badly.

It also annoyed her, she found much to her
own surprise, that she couldn't really focus on
her Walker fantasies. Which was a blessing in
disguise, she reasoned. After all, she'd decided
that absolutely no good could come of it if
they were to begin any kind of liaison, even

if he was incredibly gallant and masculine. Besides, men always leave. With no exception. That is what she was taught as a child, both from her mother's pain and from her father's actions when he left them both when Ruby was a child.

As cliché as it was, too cliché even for Ruby to face herself or seek any meaningful therapy for it, her father just up and left one day. Seemingly out of the blue. Ruby came home from school on an ordinary day feeling very neutral about the world and about having to attend school. There was nothing of note to report in those days. It was what it was. But by dinner time when her dad still wasn't home and her mum was so silent that Ruby couldn't even rouse an argument, Ruby's gut twisted in on itself with dread. Confused, Ruby went to bed willingly. Like the magic of the night would erase anything unpleasant and her dad would be there at breakfast, whistling and slurping black tea like he always had done.

She was almost afraid to wake up, especially when she heard no commotion outside her bedroom. Her mum was still in bed, lying on her side and staring at the bedroom wall. Ruby crept in and lay beside her not knowing exactly what was happening but, with the grace and naivety that can only possess a child, she knew that something terrible had happened. The heaviness of the air said so. It cut into both of their lives like a sharp knife cutting birthday cake. There was one side of the cake which was her life before her dad left and then the other side of the cake—melted, crumbling and turning mouldy— her life after her dad left. Ruby was just left with bits of inedible cake that she kept trying to fashion into something useable and liveable ever since.

When Ruby quizzed her mum about it when she left home, the pain was still visible in her eyes. Faded but still there. Her mum fobbed her off with some kind of vague suggestion that her father now lived with a new family in a beachside town across the country. Ruby didn't push, there was no point stabbing at an old wound that would bring nothing fresh and new into their lives.

The subconscious narrative that men always leave was further reinforced for Ruby when her first boyfriend, a much older Hendrick, who she met at the bookstore when she first started there, tripled backflipped on all his fervent promises to leave his wife and not only ended up staying with her but having a third baby. And, if the bookstore rumours are correct, ended up having a baby with his other side mistress that wasn't Ruby. Not only was Ruby not Hendrick's first priority in love but she wasn't even his second. Ever since, Ruby had not even bothered to pretend that love would someday be on the cards for her. It was just one constant cycle of financial woes that she was never able to get on top of. Thankfully, she had Cooper by her side which was as cliché and sad as it sounded: the straight girl and the gay guy dynamic. But Ruby was content that way. At least she thought she was until the blindsiding fantasies about dating Walker started to seep in.

As she waited for her cat scan x-rays to return, she made a firm deal with herself. In no way, no how, was she to advance her daydreams with Walker. If that meant keeping a distance and avoiding him as best as she could at work, then that is what it would take. Surely, things would simmer down after she had worked there for a while. And she could do most of her communication through Lucy. That is, of course, if she still had a job to return to after she so rudely ran away from Walker.

The radiologist talked her through her x-ray results and was pleased to pronounce that she had no damage, no concussion and barely any bruising. The friendly woman was visibly perplexed that Ruby did not share the same palpable relief.

'Sometimes, when we are under extraordinary types of stress, our brains can do funny things. Have you got a good psychologist? I can refer you to one if you like?' she offered warmly.

Ruby swallowed at the thought of forking out for a shrink who would either tell her she was a full blown nutjob or tell her she was completely fine— she wasn't sure which was worse at this stage. But she knew that that pathway would not solve her problems, which was to keep this once in a lifetime job she had been given.

'Right, that's two promises you have to keep to yourself,' Ruby told herself out loud as she left the hospital with a yellow envelope filled with scans of her brain. 'One, stay away from Walker and two, ignore the blurry vision and wobbly brain meat and keep this job.'

Ruby checked her phone to see the time and her stomach dropped. Cooper's theatre performance was on tonight and she'd just missed it. 'Fuck,' she said to an overly friendly pigeon that scuffled around her feet. Ruby started running towards the theatre, yanking her wig back into place to cover her matted flat hair.

'I'm sorry, I'm sorry...' Ruby held out her arms to Cooper as she spotted him on the steps of the community theatre. Only half of the bulb lights that surrounded the theatre sign were working but there was still something completely enchanting about the place. There were much more people there than Ruby had been expecting. A range of shapes and heights congregated on the footpath in front of the building, split off into smaller groups.

He just shrugged at her and looked around for his theatre buddies. 'It's fine.'

'No, really it's not. I'm sorry I...'

'Ruby, it's fine. It just lets me know where

we are at.' Cooper leapt off the step he was standing on and landed on the asphalt below. He nodded with his chin at someone that Ruby didn't see.

'What do you mean?' Ruby asked sincerely.

'Nothing. Look, the group are going out to celebrate. And I'm starving. Thanks for trying. I guess.' Cooper walked over to a group of four people and stood next to a short woman with red hair that sported an impeccably straight fringe. She greeted him warmly and patted him on the back, her pride obvious. Ruby watched Cooper's back dismayed and realised that he had never been this cold to her in the years that they had known each other. It stung her like the stinging nettles that lined the garden of her childhood home in Pyrite. It was as if she had eaten a whole bowl of them.

'I'm sorry,' she whispered to the air but no one heard her. But she heard something back.

'He doesn't need you anymore.' The placid voice was back and it clouded her ears.

'No! Don't say that you jerk of a voice!'

'It's true. He doesn't need you anymore. Move on.'

Ruby gulped and stormed home, unsure whether the voice was right or not. But somewhere deep down inside her she worried that it had a point.

Chapter 11

Chapter 11

Ruby made sure she was early to work the next few days. A fresh start. And she was determined to put in more effort so even if she couldn't give them the psychic answers they wanted, she could at least appear to be doing something productive.

After she had sent a brief email apologising to Walker for darting off so quickly, citing a migraine, she heaved the stack of HR files back onto her desk and started to flip through them again. This time, it was far easier to present something. Desperation had made her shrewder.

For the employees that had been there the longest, she recorded that they were very company loyal and that Crichton Enterprises had nothing to worry about. The employees that had been there less than a year, she stated that they were a higher flight risk. She hoped that Sally would not see straight through her tactic which was just stating obvious and typical human behaviour patterns.

There was one file that intrigued her, however. A file that didn't contain any information that was outstanding. The person had been there for a little over six years and received regularly good performance reports. But every time Ruby looked at it, she couldn't really see it as such. It was like a big black dot had been placed in the centre of her eye so she would have to glean information from her peripheral vision. It reminded her of an ocular migraine she experienced during her late teen years around her period.

But a black dot over the top of a file didn't really tell her anything useful anyway. So, she decided to be somewhat transparent and wrote against the employee's number in her report:

'There is something of interest to the company with this person but I'm afraid I cannot articulate what at this point. Will be required to spend more time with this file as I am not sensing the full picture here.'

This would have the added bonus of buying her more time in the job too. Just as she was feeling satisfied with her progress, Sally stormed in towards her with short sharp strides atop her mauve coloured high heels. She didn't bother to knock

'Ruby. It's time we had some input from you regarding these investors. You've had long enough.' She paused meaningfully to push her scarlet framed glasses up her severe nose.

Ruby waited for her to finish but the silence told Ruby that she already had.

'Oh. Well, the thing is... Okay, well I don't really know what to say.'

'I knew it.' Sally raised her pointy eyebrows and pressed her knitted vest down with her palms. She walked over to Ruby's makeshift desk and placed her palms down. Slowly she removed her glasses from her face and levelled her eyesight with Ruby. 'You're a bit of a joke here. And you just keep proving the point. Don't expect to have this job for much longer.'

Ruby swore she could have heard someone say 'ooff' in the not too far distance but it could have been her own mouth.

Sally was right, Ruby realised as she watched her narrow backside step out the door. *I am a joke. Not just here but in every area of my life. A sick joke. In my friendships, in my love life, in my finances...* Letting out a long, weary sigh she bargained with herself to sort herself out. Living with the promise of constantly being on the verge of being fired was making her fret and she didn't know how much longer she could take it for. Even if the money was more than she ever imagined she could earn.

As soon as she'd finished the report, Ruby spent the afternoon scouring the web for job vacancies. Of which she came up with less than before she started at Crichton Enterprises. *How on earth can that be? There has to be at least one job out there that I can do?* The air left her body.

At the end of the day, Ruby scooped up her handbag and thought of the glass of wine that she wanted to have with Cooper. Who wasn't replying to any of her texts or calls. It was clear that he was upset with her and she didn't know what she could do to make it right. The voice was obviously right, he didn't need her anymore. He had his theatre friends and his youth and a life that didn't really involve Ruby. How could it involve Ruby if she was selfish enough not to remember the things important to him and show up to support him?

On the way out, she swept past the reception desk to the other side of the offices where Walker and Sally's offices resided. Lucy wasn't around, probably left for the day after she heard him say something about getting a haircut. Ruby quickly learnt that he got his hair cut every few weeks, which showed because his hair was sleek and beautiful like a horse's tail.

'That's because I straighten it every morning, hun,' he said when she complimented him. And lifting his hand to his mouth in a stage whisper he confessed, 'and every bathroom break if you must know.' Ruby admired his dedication to style, which absolutely showed and was absolutely worth it.

To Ruby's relief, Sally wasn't around either, so she unceremoniously dumped the report and HR files on the middle of her desk. 'Make of it what you will,' she told no one.

Looking around before entering the elevator, she gave the office a cursory glance in case it was her last.

Stepping out into the first touches of evening, Ruby went to hoick her handbag over her shoulder and caught sight of the book that Cooper had given her. She looked at it with disdain. 'Some good you did.' She plucked it out of its hiding place and threw it into the bin on the footpath that separated the Crichton Enterprises building from the rest of the world. If she was going to lose the job, she was done with the acting and the pretend psychic life.

It wasn't her best decision but it was by no means her worst but Ruby was flailing and feeling a little desperate. The dour bartender semi recognised her as she walked to their favourite booth at Cynthia's. The booth seemed much larger when it was just her.

'Can I have a shot of...' Ruby wanted to say tequila. The word was dripping off her tongue but it would be no fun without Cooper. It would just be rather glum. 'Actually, make that a cider and a tap water.'

The bartender lined up the two glasses on the bar and grabbed her wheat-coloured ponytail with one hand and stroked the length of it. 'Have that for free, hun. You're always in here with that skinny kid whinging about having no money,' her thick Australian accent ricocheting off the walls.

Ruby didn't waste time sipping back a quarter of the cider before she remembered herself and thanked the bartender profusely.

'Don't sweat it. But it's not a habit, okay?'

Ruby nodded in agreement. Did the woman truly think she didn't want to afford her own drinks? 'Hey, you haven't seen that skinny kid here recently, have you?'

'No, mate,' the shiny blonde replied back and left Ruby alone to her misery and her drink.

Ruby got home late from the bar but at least she wasn't hammered. The Aussie bartender, who was actually a whole lot sweeter than Ruby had given her credit for, shouted her another drink and talked to her a bit about what she did. 'Yeah mate, I could tell you've seen some shit just by lookin' at ya.' She declared upon Ruby announcing timidly that she was a psychic.

Unwilling to really admit it, it kind of flattered Ruby. There was this stranger who, in a round about way, saw a force within her. And if it was mostly a sham, Ruby didn't really care. Who amongst the world didn't fake most of their personality and lifestyle anyway? There were international billion-dollar social media platforms dedicated to the art.

Ruby smiled as she slid into bed, after peeling off her black clothes— vowing that maybe, just maybe, she might go for a deep burgundy or grape coloured top to mix things up a bit the next day. Her hand slid out and patted her trusty wig goodnight. Despite thinking that she may be about to lose her job and her best friend wasn't talking to her but at least she was a little less invisible to the world and to a stranger tonight.

She fluffed her doona up and down to get rid of the annoying bumps that drove her mad whenever she slept. As the doona lifted into the air to fall one last time, Ruby spotted it: a small midnight blue rectangle in her bed. Squealing, she leapt out of bed in fright, holding onto herself as she cowered with her back to the wall.

'Don't be so fucking ridiculous Ruby. It's probably that box of chocolates that you fell asleep eating the other night you sick disgrace of an adult.' Comforted by her self chiding, she strolled over in nothing but a racerback singlet and underwear and yanked the doona towards her.

What lay beneath was as sinister as it was benign. Any other day, the little blue rectangle positioned squarely in her bed would not have roused a second thought. But the fact that she had thrown the psychic book away earlier that day added a menacing angle. Someone had seen her throw the book away, retrieved it from a stinky public bin, broken into her house and made certain she would see it. On some level, she was more freaked out than when she had been clubbed over the head. Lifting the book above her head, she armed herself. If the perpetrator was still in her place, she was going to lodge the book squarely in their face, no matter how threatening they seemed.

'Yo book thief, you still here?' Silence.

As a warning, Ruby threw the book across the room into her bathroom. As the book hurtled to the polished tiles, she saw scribbles across some of the pages. Hastily retrieving the book, she stood shivering in the evening light and flicking through the pages. A few places throughout the book, someone had scrawled in almost illegible handwriting: 'leave Crichton now.'

Chapter 12

Chapter 12

'Pick up, pick up, pick up. Pick up ya weirdo vampire,' Ruby said into her phone.

'Hello?' A delicate female voice answered.

'Err hi. I'm after Cooper, he about?' *How quickly I can be replaced*, Ruby thought aghast.

'Now's not a great time. Who's calling please?'

'Wait. What? Cooper has some kind of secretary now? Tell him Ruby needs him and this is an A-1 Twilight emergency,' Ruby had no idea what she meant but hoping that the urgency would be conveyed through the phone, especially as she waggled the book towards the

phone as if Cooper could see her. There was silence at the end of the line as Ruby debated
storming over to Cooper's house in the dark
and demanding she sleep on his couch in need
of safety.

The voice came back. 'Listen, Ruby.
Cooper... he can't... Tomorrow is his cousin's funeral. I'm sure he would want you to be there.
Knightsbridge Church at ten. I'll let him know
you're coming.' And with that, she rang off.

'Fuck,' Ruby said to the walls of her bedroom. 'I fucking hate funerals.' And reflecting
on her self centredness she replied to herself,
'who doesn't, dickhead?'

Tiptoeing to her fridge, she pulled out the
almost antique bottle of vodka from the freezer
that had not much more than two shots left.
At the back of her fridge, behind a tub of hum-
mus that had been expired for more than a year
and an old container of tinned beetroot, lay a
small piccolo of terrible sparkling wine. Ruby
hadn't touched it because she'd mainly forgot
about it and it was absolutely revolting. She had
never been desperate enough, even when she

was fired from the bookstore. But now, she was at the height of desperation.

Pouring the chilled vodka into a tumbler and then pouring the sparkling wine on top of it, licking it off her fingers where it sprayed outwards, she took a delicate sip. Grimacing with the vulgar taste, she took a deep breath and chucked back two large gulps. They hit her stomach satisfyingly and it didn't take long for the buzz to work its way through her body up to her head. Placing the glass down so as not to spill it, she shuffled over to her makeshift dining table and pushed it towards the door with her backside. It screeched across the floor like it was hanging onto the side of a cliff face and an evil villain was about to step on its fingers. But it did the job. Once it was positioned across the doorway, she felt somewhat safer. Which could have been the booze. For added safety and weight, Ruby hauled a few armfuls of her cherished books onto the table. Brushing off her hands like they did in cartoons, she hoped she would be safe long enough to get some sleep and that no mystery prowler would come in and return her rubbish, like someone obviously had with the book she threw away.

After downing the rest of the drink, Ruby said a quick and unorthodox prayer to the ceiling and lay down in bed, letting sleep rush its way to her.

The next morning, Ruby desperately wanted to wear her wig to the funeral. It had fast become her security blanket, her talisman of strength and helped transform her into an almost different persona. Well, she was still the same self-centred and victimised Ruby but with the wig, she seemed to have more confidence.

It sat on her bedside table, resting on an upturned bowl and she stroked it several times. 'Sorry not today, Wiggy. I have to go all ugly and bareheaded with my natural hair. At least I can legitimately wear all black.' Ruby strained her ears as she thought she heard a faraway voice tell her to wear the wig. But knew that was ludicrous and wishful thinking as the pigeons return to their warble outside her window.

'I guess it's just you and me then,' she said to the psychic book as she stuffed it back into her handbag and appraised herself in the mirror. The book sat on the bathroom floor all night whilst Ruby slept, uncannily well— thank you vodka— but in the morning she couldn't bear to leave it there. So, she plucked it from its resting spot and let it watch her get ready.

The mirror showed back to her one long line of black in her black dress, black stockings and small black ankle boots. Self-conscious of her doughy arms, she donned a cardigan even though it was too warm for her to be comfortable. It became a little sticky under her breasts as she moved the dining table and books from her doorway, undoing her safety mechanism from the night before. 'Books always save me,' she said to herself.

Using the very last of her coins that lived in a mug on top of her fridge— that were strictly for emergencies only such as food or medicine and most definitely not for cabs that she took because she couldn't be bothered using public transport— she hailed a taxi as she pressed her fingers where her bra underwires were, hoping that it would mop up some of the sweat.

'Lovely day for a funeral,' Ruby said to the cab driver who took her to the church.

'Where I come from, we don't have funerals. We just set the bodies on fire,' the cabby jeered back to her via the rearview mirror.

'Wow, really? Where do you come from?'

The cabby laughed, 'downtown, the really poor suburbs.'

'Oh, I see,' Ruby laughed too. Mostly out of discomfort and to distract herself from constantly thinking about what she was going to say to Cooper.

Nothing Ruby, she warned herself. *At the most, you say sorry for your loss and ask if he needs anything and then give him his space. That is absolutely the limit. Gottit?* She asked herself sternly. *Yeah, yeah*, she mentally replied back as if some part of her mind was a petulant teenager.

But when she stepped through the church and saw him sitting straight and composed in the second pew, she felt differently. His navy suit jacket came out wider than his bony shoulders and his hair was freshly styled, the deep fringe that he wore swept to the side was pushed back into a pompadour and styled with product. He turned when she took her pew, right at the back, as if he could sense her and looked her dead in the eye. His face looked different in such circumstances. His cheekbones lifted up his face as his skin lay across them like a big sheet of silk. There were dark streaks under his eyes but his irises shone brightly enough for Ruby to catch them all the way at the back of the church.

The front of the church boasted a traditional aesthetic. A pudgy guy in robes stood behind a thin microphone and a pulpit to the side of the stage. In the middle of the extended rostrum, was a smiling headshot the size of a surfboard and before it an enormous bouquet of white lilies which overtook the narrow table it stood upon.

The casket was surprisingly glossy and looked like honeycomb from where Ruby was stationed. It looked like it had been sawn in half, like a magic trick, and the bottom half was closed, whilst the top was peeled open. Ruby could see the creamy satin fabric that lined the open half and her initial reaction was to think of the luxurious feel it must provide. To whom, she did not know.

Sitting next to Cooper was the perky girl with the epic fringe from the theatre. Given the way she was rubbing Cooper's back in slow circles, it was obvious that it was who Ruby spoke to on the phone. And likely her new replacement.

Ruby locked eyes with Cooper and watched as beams filed upwards from his head, filled with tiny filaments of golden light. It looked like sparkles and dust were leaving his body and dispersing about a foot above his head. No one else seemed to be that concerned about it so Ruby questioned how often these messy churches get dusted. Clearly not very much. I mean, surely you could just pray the dust away if you have that kind of close connection with old mate upstairs.

To Ruby's surprise and pleasure, Cooper's mouth slowly arched upwards as he half-smiled at her. He didn't say it but Ruby could feel, through their connection that still existed, even if he was mad at her that he was grateful she was there.

Although the funeral was heartbreaking, Cooper's aunty did not make a sound or shed a tear throughout the entire procession. She sat stock-still, frozen in time, looking down at the floor, unable to look at the casket that held her dead son. At one point, she just plainly slid off her chair and onto the floor, her skirt hitching up on the way down, revealing thick grey stockings and a little bit of her underwear. Even this, which could mortify anyone over the age of twelve in an ordinary situation, did not stir her and she just sat on the floor waiting whilst the two people beside her slipped their hands under her armpits and wordlessly returned her to her seat. The stuffy celebrant glanced over her as she sat motionless on the floor but didn't even skip a beat with his address, his voice remained even, which made Ruby shudder at the clinical nature of it all. It was as if the celebrant had been through this so many times, had witnessed so much demonstrable grief that it refused to move him anymore.

Ruby kept stealing glances at Cooper to see how he was reacting. She really wanted to be seated next to him but surely it was too late to move halfway during a funeral. The unspoken rule was, like a cinema, once you've chosen your seat you're there for the duration.

As the funeral organisers set the music up through the piped speakers, a painful melodic tune from a forlorn-looking band in the late nineties, most people bowed their heads and finally let out the relief of tears into their tissue-filled hands. Which is probably why they didn't see what Ruby did. Which is just as well.

At the end of the casket, Ruby witnessed a little flicker of movement. At first, she thought it was a large moth that had comically made its way into the service. But the moth got bigger and before long, Ruby noticed it was a shoe. A foot to be exact, wiggling and flickering as if someone was trying to shake off their pins and needles. The foot, in a formal black laced up shoe, was followed by a suit leg, followed by a thin greying hand that snaked its fingers over the side of the casket.

Ruby looked around in a panic wondering if this was some kind of joke. Were people around her laughing or crying? Nobody was roused by the fact that the dead body in the casket was flipping its limbs about. The rotund celebrant continued to stand at the pulpit with his eyes closed in prayer, unaware of the supernatural wonder that was happening before him.

From the back of her mind, she remembered something about bodies moving during rigor mortis and vehemently decided it had to be that.

But what happened next was definitely not rigor mortis as the thin hand-pulled himself up and revealed a confused face. He shook his head, the mop of raven black hair flopping either side of his head. Ruby could do nothing but stare in awe at what was happening before her. Did someone make a mistake? Was he not dead after all? Thank goodness that he wasn't buried alive. But everyone in the church continued to mourn to the maudlin soundtrack that echoed throughout the hall. No one stirred.

Cooper's cousin caught Ruby's eye and pointed a reedy finger at her. 'You,' he mouthed.

'Me?' Ruby mouthed back, pointing a finger back at herself. The cousin rolled his eyes at her and beckoned her to him with that same unsettling finger.

'I can't,' she mouthed whilst holding up her hands and shrugging. The person next to her cleared his throat and looked at her through one open eye.

The corpse rolled his eyes at her again and beckoned her with his head. Shutting her eyes and pressing her lips together, Ruby slowly crept down the aisle towards the casket trying not to make a sound and draw attention to herself or the talking corpse.

She grimaced when she went past Cooper and he glared at her but surely she had to help this young man get out of the casket, right? She had no choice. The brain scan showed there wasn't anything physically wrong with her, so it couldn't be a brain tumour or anything. Even if she was having a little psychological slip-up, she could always pass it off as wanting to pay her respects to the body. Of some guy she never met.

'Fucking took you long enough,' the cousin said to her. He didn't quite look dead but he barely looked alive either. Ruby had a feeling that's how he looked when he was alive anyway, judging by the traces of his emo look that still remained.

Ruby didn't answer, especially as the priest was giving her a weird side-eye. 'Look, I think you're the only one here who can see me. And I need someone to know that it wasn't a heart attack that I died of. It was drugs. I took too much meth, see...' he hooked his lip up with a finger to reveal a gap where some teeth were missing. 'Meth is revolting. But I really need you to tell my mum that I didn't kill myself intentionally and it wasn't a heart attack from her buying me that treadmill, which I never used by the way but I just told her that I had started using it to appease her. Anyway, point of the story is: it wasn't anyone's fault but my own. Cooper needs to stop blaming himself. And I absolutely need you to get that message to my folks. Can you do that?'

Ruby had entirely no intention or no way of knowing how to do that but despite herself, she nodded vigorously at the talking corpse.

'Thanks, Red. Oh and talk to Cooper. You two are... special.' The cousin winked at Ruby and flopped back into the casket dramatically, his paper-thin hands falling across his chest and a smile spreading on his face.

After the funeral formalities, Cooper sidled up to Ruby who was waiting under a luxurious willow tree out the front of the church. 'What in the fuck was that, Ruby?'

Ruby feigned innocence. 'What? Just checking out a dead body. It's a totally normal and appropriate response.'

Cooper shook his head and placed it in his hands. Ruby could feel how heavy and burdened he felt and was compelled to lift the weight off him. She cared so deeply about her best friend and perhaps the only person in her life, besides her mum, that she would move mountains for.

'Hey, so listen. I'm probably, most likely... okay definitely going nuts but I have to tell you something. Promise not to judge me?'

'I absolutely will judge you, you fabulous weirdo,' he said without a beat.

Even though his face and voice were deadpan, Ruby felt a wave of relief come over her. He still cared about her too and their friendship was not over. Ruby could recover things. Unless he reacted badly to what she was about to say.

'So, when I was having a little peekaboo at the open casket...'

'Smack bang in the middle of the funeral ceremony... hmmm, yeah I remember.' Cooper said drily.

'Yes, then. Welp, your cuz started talking to me. From his casket. During his funeral. Whilst he was dead.' As she said it out loud, she realised what a complete and utter fool she sounded like and desperately wished she could suck those words back in and pretend that today never happened.

'Heh. What did he say then? That he loves bad emo music?'

Ruby snorted with laughter and several grievers turned sharply to look at the pair under the willow tree. Cooper waved them off dismissively.

'He said... he said that he didn't die of a heart attack. That he was a meth head. And that everyone should stop blaming themselves, especially you.'

Cooper was silent and Ruby's gut twisted.

'I'm sorry. That's so fucked. I shouldn't have said that. I need a shrink. I'll book one today,' she backpedalled.

Cooper removed his skinny tie. 'Ruby, I was the only one who knew he did meth. I've been beating myself up for not getting him help sooner. His parents have been saying he died from a heart attack, which is kind of true but I know full well that he overdosed on meth.'

'Fuck,' was all Ruby could say as the pair sat in grim silence waiting for the other person to move or say something.

After they sat like that for the length of a sitcom episode and Ruby had chewed away most of the quick around her fingernails, she decided it was time to go for broke. 'There are other things as well. My vision keeps going blurry and I'm hearing voices— well a voice— and I got hit in the head and someone left me a threatening note and...' Ruby took a huge breath and blurted out all the paranormal happenings that she couldn't explain. 'Ever since I've pretended to be a psychic, it's like... well... I'm becoming kinda psychic.'

'I've heard that often happens. Once you acknowledge the possibility, it makes room for it to come through,' Cooper said evenly. Ruby was shocked that he didn't run away or look at her like she was crazy. He was just so accepting of all the weird stuff that she had blurted out.

'How do you know this?' Ruby half turned her torso and grabbed his shoulder.

'Well, if you turned up to my theatre show like you'd promised you would know. I played a psychic and have been researching myself into a hole these past few months. The book I gave you was mine that I ordered in from the shop. I thought you might find it useful. And here we are.'

'Here we are,' Ruby said glumly. The insides of her throat stuck together as she pushed past it to offer the apology she should have offered up earlier. 'Look, I'm really sorry I missed your theatre show. I should have put in more of an effort. I know how much it means to you and I have been so wrapped up in my own whirlwind of nonsense that I put you on the backburner. I shouldn't ever do that, especially cos you're my favourite vampire in the whole world and you never even bite me!' Ruby playfully punch his arm.

'Oh hilarious. Just because I have almost see-through skin...' He trailed off and they both noticed the grieving crowd had dispersed, the celebrant who looked like a big purple grape in his robes that matched the colour of his jowls pulled the wooden doors shut towards him.

'It's fine, I'm over it. But will you come to the next one?'

Ruby held up a palm to him. 'Oohh, I'm sorry I can't I'm busy that night getting another brain Xray,' she laughed heartily at her own joke.

'Very funny. Wait... you had a brain scan?'

'Yes, ya little superstar. That's where I was when I missed your thespian debut, which isn't an excuse because I also forgot about it. Nothing to worry about though,' she wrapped her head with her knuckles, 'everything seems to be in order up here in my stomach. Wait... nope that's not it. Is it my liver? Brain! That's it, that's what goes here,' she said jokingly as she pointed to her head.

'Cut it out, you corpse loving freak. I can't tell if you're joking or not. So, what were the results? Do we need to get some post lobotomy activewear at the ready?'

'I know you're kidding but that actually sounds delightfully comfortable. We could start our own clothing line. Call it "lobotowear" or something? Anyway, yes, I'm completely fine. According to my little black and white pictures. Which, is actually more troubling than it sounds.'

'Oh? How so?'

'It means that it's either a psychological wear down or I really am turning a bit psychic. And, frankly, I do not know which is more terrifying.'

'Oh, Ruby. How's your general mood? Any appetite changes?'

'My mood is borderline petulant almost always and I think about wine a lot.'

'So absolutely zero changes there. Close your eyes for a sec.'

'Oh Edward, do I dare trust you?' Ruby said melodramatically.

'Do it. And may I remind you that we are still at my cousin's funeral, so if you could kindly keep it down.'

Ruby obeyed Cooper's instructions and fluttered her eyelids closed. With her eyes shut, she felt the inside of her head buzz a little but nothing that caused alarm.

'Right, now I'm going to ask a question and I want you to say the very first answer that springs up to mind, okay? No second-guessing or overthinking, it has to genuinely be the first answer, even if you feel like it's the wrong one.'

'Gotchya. If it's about what we should get to eat, I can save you some time as I already know that it's dumplings.' Ruby lifted an eyebrow and peered through one half-open eye at Cooper.

'Chill, we'll grab some after. Now close your eyes...' Cooper swiped his warm hand over Ruby's eyes about an inch away from her skin. Ruby could feel the warmth shoot straight through her eyelids to the back of her brain. It was like stepping into a tepid bath and she wanted more of it.

'Okay, do you think you are going crazy or you are psychic? First answer: go!'

'Psychic.' Ruby's eyes flew open and she clasped a hand to her mouth. She was not expecting that answer to come out of her mouth. But now that it had, she released how much pressure she had been holding. The potential threat of being mentally unwell was teetering before her and now that she'd acknowledged that it was unlikely that, she felt more at peace and less afraid of falling into a deep, dark pit.

'And there you go.' Cooper smiled smugly.

'Could I really be?' Ruby looked around her as it sunk it. Like a Rolodex flipping its pages, realisations started to fall in her mind and things started to make sense. 'I guess it explains all these weird arse happenings. The corpse. The visions at work. How about the other day, I was chatting to my boss at work, well his heart kinda broke and bled in front of me.'

'Hang on, that reminds me... you got a death threat?'

'Oh yeah, that. The whole psychic thing doesn't explain that. First, someone broke into my apartment and smacked me over the head. Hence why I got a brain scan...'

Cooper cut her off, 'what the actual fuck, Ruby? What did the police say?'

'Erm. They were very polite. And by polite I mean, silent. And by silent, I mean I didn't go to the police station.'

'Ruby! We're going right this minute.'

'No, no, no! It's too late now and really what are they going to do to help? Tell me to put a better lock on the door or move apartments? Nothing was taken and my brain is *turtle-y fine.*'

'Anyone who says "turtle-y fine" is not fine in my opinion but alas.'

'And, if you remember correctly, the last time something bad happened to me I got fired from my job. So I can't exactly trust people of authority now, can I?'

'I see where you're coming from but... what about the book?'

'Oh yeah, so I'm going to rock up to a police station and show them a book about becoming a psychic. And the writing says to leave Crichton now and then I have to explain I work there as a consulting psychic and they are going to be like...' Ruby threw her hands up in despair.

'I'm walking you home. And promise me

that you'll seriously think about going to the police. I'll even come with you!'

'Hold up, I thought I was promised dumplings?'

Cooper stood up and held his hand out to Ruby. His skin was an unusual mixture of warm and cool and Ruby took it with enthusiasm. 'Come on then, Little Miss Psychic. Tell me, can you foretell my future? How many dumplings will I buy you?'

'The answer is in the stars, Cooper. Obviously.' She rolled her eyes in exaggeration but couldn't help feeling glad that she was with her best friend again.

As they both slurped up flimsy dumplings at a pokey little dumpling house where they occasionally had lunch when they worked together at the bookstore, Ruby couldn't help smiling. She watched the way Cooper's rectangular eyebrows jumped up with each bite of dumpling. 'Hey, I gotta ask you something, Edward.'

'Shoot.'

'Did you have a little sip-sip of tequila this morning? No judgement from this side of the dumpling house but I was just wondering.'

'Um, no. I'm not a boozehound like you and am perfectly capable of attending a mid-morning funeral without getting comfortably numb, thank you.'

'Alright, I said no judgement!' She waved her serviette at him. 'It's just that I can really smell tequila. It's like you're wearing it as a perfume,' she looked to the distance. 'Wait, is that a thing? Tequila perfume? Should we sell it?' After thinking about it for a short second, she shook her head with her own ridiculousness. 'No, that's silly. Of course not.'

'I'm not wearing tequila perfume and I can't smell anything. Maybe it's the soy sauce you've got dribbled all down your front. And in your hair. And in the corner of your mouth,' Cooper looked down to her hands. 'Oh and in your fingernails too. Sheesh, woman.'

Ruby grinned and sucked at her fingers with no care for decorum in front of the person she felt the most comfortable with. 'Nope, not tequila. Just good old salty goodness.'

'Right, I'll pay and walk you home. Then I've gotta head over to my aunt's and do post-funeral family stuff. I should be there by now actually,' Cooper stood up and checked that his tie was still in his pocket and slung his suit jacket back over his delicate shoulders.

But Ruby didn't want to be apart from him. 'Not even time for a cheeky bevvy at Cynthia's on the way? I mean, we walk right past it so it would be rude not to.'

'No Ruby. Not today. You're obsessed with Tequila! Don't tell me you have a drinking problem as well. I don't want to have to see you rise up in your casket any time soon.'

They walked along the sidewalk in comfortable silence, Cooper with his hands in his pockets and swinging his torso side to side, neither in a huge hurry to do whatever they had to do next. Between them, lingered something magical in its own right. Something that travelled somewhere between comfort and excitement. And to Ruby, it was addictive. Maybe she should give up the ruse of this consulting psychic caper and beg for her bookstore job back? And then she remembered something. Halting in the middle of the sidewalk she turned to Cooper and exclaimed, 'Oh my goodness, so I'm like actually psychic?'

Cooper good-naturedly laughed at her. 'I guess so.'

'We have to try it out properly sometime, like if I just concentrate all my efforts, surely I can see things? Here, let's try with you.' She grabbed both his hands and shut her eyes. But Cooper shook them off hastily. 'No thanks, keep your wizardry away from me thanks. Save it for your workplace.'

Ruby pouted but hardly thought Cooper was fair game anyway. She basically knew everything about him.

'Are you sure you haven't accidentally spilt tequila on your pants or something? It's really strong,' Ruby waved her hand in front of her nose.

'What kind of slob do you think I am Ruby?' But Cooper was talking to her back as she ran off up the street away from him. 'Ruby?'

Ruby sprinted right up to the door of Cynthia's and stood outside. She swore she could hear someone yelling 'help' from inside. But as she got closer there was no yelling.

'Ruby, I said that we are not drinking today,' Cooper declared as he caught up with her.

'No, no listen.' Both stood still and listened but nothing happened. Ruby placed both hands up to the door and as soon as she touched them, she was jolted back like an electric zap went through her. The smell of tequila was now so strong that she covered her nose and mouth with her arm.

'What's going on, Ruby? Is this an elaborate skit to get me to buy you wine or is this a psychic thing?' Cooper looked almost worried.

'Psychic thing. Something is happening inside here. The door's locked though. Help me try and bust it open.'

Cooper looked down at his frail arms and legs and his noticeable lack of strength and just shrugged at Ruby.

'Fine,' she said. Let's go around the back and see if there is another entrance.

Down the side alley, there was a smaller unmarked brown door that was, thankfully, unlocked. It led to a stairwell that stank of stale urine and Cooper started to have misgivings. 'Ruby, I'll wait outside.'

'Like fuck you will. Come on, the bar is this way,' and she led the way into Cynthia's which was almost in pitch darkness except for the glow of the neon sign that was always on in the window. It was unusual that there were no patrons given that it was quickly closing in on night time.

'They're obviously closed. Hope we don't get busted for trespassing.'

'Shhh,' Ruby whispered urgently as she noticed the bottles of spirits shudder and wobble in the glass shelves behind the bar. 'Look!' She pointed to the bottles and as she did, a bottle of tequila shimmied its way to the edge of the ledge and toppled off. The crash and the pungent smell of the spirit hitting them all at once.

'Tequila!' They both shouted. Ruby went to race towards the offending bottle but Cooper struck out a hand to stop her.

'Hold up, it was probably a small earthquake. Or, poltergeist activity. Do poltergeists exist? Now that you're psychic?'

But Ruby had ducked underneath his arm and was leaning over the top of the bar. 'Cooper, come quick!' She shouted but he was already by her side. Ruby swung around to the back of the bar all whilst Cooper dialled for an ambulance before they had a chance to think.

Chapter 13

Chapter 13

Chapter 13

'I can't thank you guys enough, really.' Ana, the once dour bartender sat on a barstool with a blanket wrapped around her and a cold glass of water at her helm and an icepack on the pack of her neck. The ambulance had been and gone and pronounced her harm free but suggested she take the rest of the night off.

'It must be a full moon. I rarely have fainting spells anymore, it's fairly under control. But when I was a kid, at every full moon I would have one or two. I'm so glad you found me, it can be fatal if I choke on my vomit. What a way to go, eh! Rockstar.' Ana had the charm to laugh at herself. Cynthia's owner had rushed down not long after and had cleaned up the tequila and offered both Cooper and Ruby a bottle each in gratitude.

'How the flip did you know what was goin' on though? Could you see through the window?' Ana was flummoxed

'You see, our girl Ruby is—' Cooper began but Ruby cut him off.

'It was just a hunch really. Unusual for the bar to be closed at this time of day. And, we were just really desperate for a drink,' she winked at Cooper.

'Oh, that's right. You're psychic. Cheers to your hunches eh, Ruby?' Ana lifted her glass of water towards them both and sipped gingerly.

By the time Cooper walked Ruby home, it was dark except for the full moonlight that bathed both of them. Ruby was buzzed but Cooper was exhausted. She could tell by how much the indents under his eyes had deepened and darkened. There was an almost maternal part of her that wanted to reach out and swipe her thumb across them.

'You be alright to get home on your own,

or you wanna crash in my bed with me?' She asked him tenderly.

'And have you do your dumpling farts on me all night? No thanks. I'll call you tomorrow,' Cooper leant in and stroked one side of her head affectionately and the safe, comforting feeling that he produced returned to Ruby again. She watched the bottom of his suit jacket swing from side to side as he walked away, leaving her at the front of her apartment building. Something, just a little twinge, barely noticeable, felt a little sad inside of her as he was leaving. It wasn't so much sadness as it was a desire for him to stay beside her. She took it as a reminder not to take him for granted anymore.

Again, shuffling the book laden table in front of the door, Ruby flopped into bed expecting to crash immediately given that she had a full belly of dumplings and an even fuller day of emotions. But despite the great sleep the night before, Ruby lay awake unable to sleep, the full moon lighting up her apartment and her mind. Thoughts went racing through her head like a school carnival, shouting and yelping begging for attention.

Along with the events of the day: talking to a dead guy, saving someone's life, realising she was a psychic, it was like the floodgates had officially opened and messages were coming in left, right and centre. Nothing that she could really make sense of but there was a heap of jumbling and rambling snippets of conversations in an array of voices. Each piece of dialogue banged around her head and banged into one another, like it was a busy shopping mall that had no exit.

Frustrated that she had no alcohol in the house and no TV to turn up to drown then out, she clenched her fists and banged them into the mattress, screwing her face up in anguish. 'Shut up! Shut the flip up!' She yelled to the ceiling.

It worked. The voices died down almost instantly and she was left with the buzz of the day's events. Ruby rolled off her bed and searched through her handbag. The book, now tainted with someone's scrawling, was still there so she thought she may as well put it to good use. Flipping through to the index she searched for 'noisy head syndrome.' *Okay, well that doesn't exist*, she thought to herself. But she did find a chapter on communicating with your guides. This will have to do, she thought.

'Right. Good. Thank you. Now, I don't mean to be ungrateful but I simply can't hear you all at once, so I'm going to have to take this bit by bit. One at a time. Can I please have a guide come forth for me now?'

And Ruby waited patiently but nothing happened. She rolled her eyes at the absurdity. It was either noisy chaos or nothing at all.

And as her body fell heavy into the mattress and let go of the events of the past few weeks, Ruby thought she heard a faraway voice say 'peer into the shiny black surface.'

Chapter 14

Chapter 14

It was mid-afternoon when Ruby awoke, her heart jumping a little until she realised it was a Sunday and she didn't have to be at work. She rose from her bed feeling heavenly with a new sense of clarity and refreshment as some peace had found its way to her. It was the first time she'd felt this way since working at the bookstore.

'Right!' She told herself. 'It's time to get serious about this malarkey.' Automatically, she reached for her black jeans and a black fitted t-shirt before remembering that she had a choice of what to wear. There was no one to impress today. So she chose a sunflower yellow wrap dress and put her natural hair up into a messy bun. With some gold hooped earrings that hung down to her chin, she felt like a new person. One that had sorted most of her problems and had a paycheque on its way. *Is* this *what it feels like to be somewhat together?* she thought smugly.

When she reached the small shop with the lilac painted façade, she hesitated before going in. Looking over both shoulders, she hoped that no one was watching her and then realised that she barely knew anyone in the city, let alone in the neighbourhood and she boldly strode across the threshold. The door chimed baldly as she stepped into Gloria's Spirit.

Instantly, the thick waft of incense— a dusty, earthy smell— came at her and she politely tried not to succumb to a cough. The shop was so packed with things that she could barely move face-first down the aisle towards the counter. In fact, she kind of had to shimmy sideways whilst pretending to look at the trinkets of miniature silver elephants, clear glass bowls of tumbled crystals and racks and racks of colourful tunics.

'Hi, love,' came a croak from somewhere behind the counter.

'Hi! Just browsing thanks.'

The middle-aged lady looked down through her glasses which sat at the end of her nose at her. When she tipped her chin down, Ruby could see that despite dying her hair an amethyst colour, she was thinning significantly at the top. And a russet brown blouse waterfalled down her shoulderless arms. At Ruby's response, she half laughed and half coughed and Ruby felt intimidated and self-conscious. Ruby went to adjust her wig and realised she didn't have it on and blushed at the lack of her safety blanket.

Trailing her fingers over a small packet of Rider-Waite tarot cards she looked around to see what she needed. Trying to remember exactly why she was here other than feeling like she needed some sort of guidance. Or some answers to her newfound abilities.

'Need some help, love?' The woman, who

Ruby could only assume was named Gloria, cawed at her.

'I... err... don't know what I need exactly. I'm sort of new to the... I'm new to all this and don't know where to start.'

Gloria leapt off her stool and the floorboards creaked below her. She placed her hands down on the glass countertop that separated them and as she did so, Ruby heard the staccato of the six different types of rings she wore bang down.

'What kinda stuff you into, love?'

'Well, that's the thing. I'm not really sure. Have you got a starter kit for psychics?'

The woman croak-laughed again. 'Nah but let me see what I can find.' Gloria stood still for a bit staring at Ruby, not even attempting to move.

'Are you... err... looking with your sixth sense?' Ruby twirled her finger around, proud of her joke and expecting to get another croak-laugh out of her. But the woman's face fell deadpan and Ruby felt silly.

Without moving from behind the counter she said, 'You'll need a tarot deck... that's what you've got there in your hand. You'll probably need a crystal ball or some kind of scrying mirror,' she waved her arm over at the wall of shelves that Ruby hadn't even got to yet. 'And you'll need some sage to burn. Everyone needs sage.'

Ruby turned the box of tarot cards over and over in her hands, they felt good to hold and gave her something tangible to pin her whole newfound world and gift on. A physical talisman that she could project onto and to help separate her identity from the voice and the visions that she had.

The woman plodded over to the shelf and picked up a gleaming black scrying mirror, which looked a lot like a stoneware cheese serving board or a blanked out handmirror.

'Wow, that must be why my...' Ruby hesitated before realising where she was. 'That's probably why I keep getting messages about a black shiny surface!' She was amazed. The more she experienced with her psychic-ness, the more it kept being proven.

'Oh yeah, what else did it say to buy in my store?' The woman pulled down her glasses a little and waited until Ruby looked her in the eye. And then she winked and it made Ruby fall into a bit of a delirious giggle.

'I actually have to be honest with you. I'm really skint and can't afford anything. Can I hold these aside when I get my pay? Which should be...' Ruby did the mental calculations... 'in about a week's time!'

'Listen, love, we don't get a lot of young ones like you in here anymore. Usually desperate divorcees like myself, you know? Perhaps I can gift them to you in exchange for a little favour? Nothing too onerous, just handing out a bunch of flyers for the shop, wherever you see fit.'

'Wow, really? Yes, that would be a huge help. Thank you.'

'You seem the good sort. Like you won't chuck the flyers straight in the bin on the way out. But who knows, darling. I'm no psychic. I'm a fraud— just like all of us!' The shop owner laughed at herself all the way back to behind the counter where she retrieved two-inch stack of envelope sized flyers which heralded ghastly yellow, blue and red text.

The thing is though, Ruby thought to herself, *that I'm not a fraud at all*. But she had no intention of ruining the good deal she struck with the lady.

The woman dropped the tarot cards, the scrying mirror, the flyers and a thick bundle of sage into a purple paper bag and handed it across the counter to Ruby, who gratefully took the string handles between her pinched fingers.

'I really appreciate this. You're not just helping me, you're helping others. I'm totally going to help people with my insights. In fact, I've already started to,' Ruby boasted to a bemused Gloria.

It felt really good to help someone and Ruby was awash with redemption after the adrenalin wore off from helping Ana. Knowing that being of the psychic persuasion and that it was actually useful gave her a jolt. A buzz. A thrill. Although it sure was going to be exhausting if she went around playing superhero to everyone in her neighbourhood. But so far, the benefits of this talent had wiped out the fear from the weird voices and strange experiences. She considered that she could even handle the apartment intruders on occasion. Maybe.

The woman laughed yet again but this time it had a harder edge to it. 'Good for you, darlin'. But I wouldn't be lying if I heard that every time a fresh psychic comes in here before they find themselves burnt out or in danger in some way or the other. Look after yourself, is all I'm saying.' She held up her mottled hands in defeat.

'Speaking of that. Do you have any ideas on how I can protect my apartment a little better? I can't afford a stronger bolt lock until the pay comes in...'

'Ahh, now we're talking. Take a leaf out of an old witch's book: scatter a line of pure white salt across the helm of your doorway. Draw a big cross across the top of your door frame—you can use string or tape if you have an antsy landlord. And you can pop some rosemary pot plants, one either side, of your doorway. Witch's salt works best.' The woman whipped around quicker than Ruby thought her body would allow and retrieved a coffee cup-sized amber jar of salt flakes that were so big they looked edible. 'But if you run out, ordinary salt will do the trick.' She plopped the jar into the bag along with her other stuff.

'That's amazing. Thank you. I'm going to tell everyone I know to shop here.'

'A lot of people is it?' The woman laughed at her own joke again and Ruby found herself warming to the woman so much more than she first had and not even because of the free stuff. 'Just kidding, love. Spread those flyers around for me, in letterboxes or community notice-boards and I will be as happy as a pig in poo. See ya, love.'

Ruby felt her heart warm and expand as she heard the door's jingle behind her. The hot Sunday afternoon spread out before her and she looked up and down the street as she decided what to do next. People seemed shinier and happier: there were cars going slower in the road, a few couples walking hand in hand and cafes had their outdoor tables all lined up where bright groups of people were enjoying coffee, pastries and big glossy bowls of pasta.

Ruby's head and body felt great. But she couldn't deny that there was a dreadful feeling at the base of her stomach. It felt like someone had a cheesegrater and was grating away the inside of her stomach lining. She didn't have to be a psychic to know that something wasn't right.

Chapter 15

Chapter 15

Ruby put the uneasy feeling down to lack of sleep and adjusting to her new life as a telepathic helpmate. After all, her enthusiasm and optimism to go to work were palpable, especially when she no longer had to fake her skills.

As she neared the reflective, stately building of Crichton Enterprises she admired her reflection. More and more she felt like she was owning the wig and loved how she felt in the sleekness of her almost all-black outfits. For once, she even skimmed her eyes over the chunkier parts of her body that she didn't like and was able to ignore them for a hot second, enough to give herself some approval for once. Life wasn't perfect but she felt like she was coming back on an even keel— like the end of a see-saw returning to centre.

A smile wiggled across her lips the entire ride up the elevator and even as she made herself the hottest coffee she could in the staff room. The warmth from the mug seeped through to the palms of her hands as she tried to shake off the weekend's final dredges of tiredness. With a new resolution, she had decided that if they were going to fire her then so be it. But until then, she would act as if she was a valuable part of the team and her job wasn't in jeopardy. For until she was fired, she wasn't going anywhere. And she felt particularly motivated to prove herself, even if she didn't know how just yet.

'Morning!' She cheerily rang out to anyone who was within earshot which, she noticed, was nobody.

Remembering the report she left on Sally's desk before the weekend, she felt trepidation as she tiptoed towards her office. Outside her office, Lucy's open-air cubicle was empty. His chair tucked neatly under the desk but Ruby thought she could faintly smell his mossy cologne.

She lingered for a bit, waiting for him to come in so they could gossip about the weekend but after five minutes he didn't show. Eager to get stuck into some work and impress both Sally and Walker with her more refined abilities, she bravely knocked on Walker's office door.

'Oh Ruby, you're here. Thank goodness.' Walker said when he plucked the door open for her. Inside his office, Sally sat on the floor— her high heels next to her and her back against the wall. It startled Ruby to see her in such casual disarray as all she knew of Sally was an uptight and sceptical woman who stalked around in deep-hued suits. Ruby wasn't even sure that she'd witnessed Sally go to the bathroom at any point.

Walker beckoned Ruby into his office with his hand but didn't offer her a seat. 'You haven't heard from Lucy by any chance, have you?'

'No. Not since we had lunch on Thursday. Is everything okay?'

Walker looked ashen and glanced at Sally. Suddenly, Ruby's disquiet stomach made sense.

'I'm worried,' Sally whispered from her reclining spot on the floor. With the softness of her voice there was a softness in her being and Ruby felt a generous compassion.

Ruby looked around where to position herself and chose a leather chair on wheels that sat opposite Walker's desk. She crab walked the chair closer to Sally as a demonstration of solidarity and took a deep breath. 'What's wrong? And, importantly, what can I do?' Ruby let out the breath through her mouth, the air whistling out.

'We haven't seen Lucy since Thursday and he hasn't called in sick. Which is highly unusual for an employee of his calibre. In fact, I think Sal and I worked out that he has taken a maximum of three days off in the six years that he has been here. And they were called in. He's not answering his phone and I've sent my driver around to knock on his door with no success. I'm sure there's no cause for alarm yet. He could simply have the flu and thought he had informed us.' Walker picked up his mobile and glanced to see if there were any new notifications. 'It's just... highly unusual.'

'Something is wrong. I just know it.' Sally said without looking anyone in the eye. Her voice was shaky and it unnerved Ruby. She watched as Sally rang Lucy again with no luck. 'Dammit.' Sally said and dropped her phone to the floor like it was too hot to touch. She jiggled her top foot, which was crossed over one ankle in front of her and shook her hands out in distress.

'I guess I can help,' Ruby offered nervously. She felt the exact kind of fraud that she felt on her first day. It was one thing to hear a few voices here and there but to locate a potentially missing person? People who have been professional psychics for most of their lives weren't even able to successfully do that at times.

Sally crawled across to her on her hands and grabbed Ruby's knees, her hands like icy clamps. She looked almost pathetic. 'Please.

Anything you can do to help. He means a lot to me.'

'Sure. I can also help with his workload too. It must be slowing you down not having an assistant.' Ruby had assumed that Lucy meant a lot to her because she felt out of control without the high level of organisation and meticulousness that she was used to with Lucy by her side. So when Sally said, 'no, it's not that at all. I don't care about work today,' Ruby almost choked on her tongue.

'I hate to state the obvious but have you called the police?' Ruby queried Walker.

'Yes, but they weren't super interested unless a family member calls in. And, as it turns out, all Lucy's emergency contacts were fake. I don't even know where to begin looking for his family members. He's not even on social media which was surprising to learn.'

'That's my fault,' Sally admitted. 'I alluded to the fact that employees that want to be taken seriously here— with the subtext of a potential promotion— need to have no social media presence.' She cringed at herself. 'I know it was stupid but we just can't risk our data and findings being vulnerable. Don't you agree, Walker?'

'There is that. But, and HR would have me say this, there's no requirement for an employee to not have a social media presence to work here.'

'Shit. This is all my fault,' Sally dipped her head into her hands and Ruby watched her manicured pink nails scratch lightly at her face.

'No, don't talk like that. It's no one's fault. Especially not because you encouraged him to stay off social media!' Walker earnestly affirmed.

With a bit of quick thinking, Ruby said 'I need an item of his and I will see what messages I can divine. It's surely just some misunderstanding.'

Walker quickly trotted off to get something from Lucy's desk. It wasn't just the way he elegantly ran that impressed Ruby but it was the way he was so eager to help one of his staff. He didn't have much of the usual standoffish, hierarchal CEO vibe that was expected. He acted like Lucy was his own assistant.

Pulling herself together, Sally pushed herself up off one bent knee and took an audible deep breath. Balancing delicately on one foot, like a steady flamingo, she slid her shoes back on. 'Right, well. Me flailing around like an emotional chook isn't going to do anything to get Lucy to work.' And just like that her trademark stoicism and stride returned as she headed out of Walker's office. As she reached the doorway, she turned back to Ruby and demanded, 'you need to find him, Ruby. This is serious.'

Ruby nodded in response but the chill on Sally's words left her uneasy. And very much doubting that she could do anything. Especially since she hadn't heard the nice feminine voice that encircled her head for a few days now. All her other psychic senses had seemed to be heightened, however. Hearing the corpse talk, smelling the tequila, the feeling in the pit of her stomach that something was amiss... they had come out of nowhere almost at the same time now that she had opened the channel to her new way of being. And, she had to admit, she was grateful for them. If they had happened at any other time in her life, she was not sure that she would have been so welcoming. There must be something in this divine timing thing that all these books and experts keep pertaining to, she confirmed with herself.

Not long after, Walker rushed back into his office holding a little round tin of lip balm. 'Was all I could find,' he said apologetically as he handed it over to Ruby. She turned it over in her hands and looked up to see Walker eagerly eyeballing her.

'Right. Sorry. I'll...' Walker leant back and indicated he would leave.

'Don't be silly. This is your office. I'll be in the boardroom for a minute and I'll let you know if anything pops up.'

The lip balm stared back at her. If it had eyelids it wouldn't be blinking. It gave nothing away. She shook it for good luck. Nothing. 'Come on you little jerk.' She said to it which didn't help. No voices, no smells and no visions. Nothing was happening. Her psychic skills had all but vanished in her time of need. Why did they randomly appear? More importantly, how could she control them?

Sliding her shoes off, she tip-toed to the helm of the boardroom door and stuck her head out to make sure no one was around. When she saw that the coast was clear she quickly ducked back in and grabbed her phone.

'Coops. We have a situation.'

'Listening,' he said back to her through the speaker.

'Okay, so this guy from work, Lucy, is apparently missing and the bosses want me to like, I don't know find him or something. Use my "powers", she said with disparagement. 'What should I do?'

'Wait, you mean they want you to do the job they actually hired you for?'

'I knowww,' she whined. 'It's so rude of them.'

'But aren't you the real deal now?'

'I thought I was after this weekend but nothing seems to be happening. It's like it has all stopped. Someone turned off the switch.'

'Can it work like that?'

'How would I know? You're the psychic expert.'

'Hey, I just read some books and played one in a community theatre production that barely thirty people— which didn't include your fine self— saw.'

'Sheesh, are you still holding that one against me? I was in hospital, remember?'

'Just playing with ya, Ruby. I've gotta have something over you, otherwise you'll use your witchy powers against me and read all my deep and dark thoughts and extort me!'

'Yeah, I'm bound to. I couldn't think of anything more boring that sifting through your catalogues and catalogues of thoughts about men on horseback in the nude.'

'Ruby do you think that's what I find attractive? Do you think anyone finds that attractive?'

'Umm hello, isn't that what *Brokeback Mountain* is about?'

'I wouldn't know. I've never actually seen it. Too young.'

'Oof. Way to make a lady feel old. All I can think about is, don't they get sweaty bumcrack juice all over the saddle when they're riding? And where does their doodle go? Does it just bounce along, smacking onto the saddle when they ride?' Ruby stared off into the distance, contemplating the logistics of naked cowboys.

'Ruby. Jeez.'

'What! Don't tell me you've never thought about it.'

'I've never thought about it. Now can I go or do you want to make me squirm a little bit more?'

'Help me! What do I do? How do I kickstart my psychic game again to help find my co-worker? It's not just that my bosses will have my guts for garters if I don't contribute at least something but he was my only friend here.'

'Well, what were you doing when you have had the incidences, sorry visions, in the past?'

'Let's see. There was the funeral... then the tequila thing. Both of those things I were looking at you. Hooley dooley. You're my missing amulet! The hero of my life. The yin to my yang. The soy sauce to my dumplings.' Ruby stifled a giggle.

'Will that be all? There's actually a customer in here.'

'Wait! I'll be serious now. There's no rhyme or reason. It has just seemed to happen.'

'I would be looking for patterns. Must be the Virgo in me. What things trigger your insights and flashes? And then try to replicate them. Or you can use the tools you got from the hippy shop.'

'Good idea! You kinda are like my hero.' Ruby swore she could feel the heat of Cooper blushing through the phone.

'I gotta go flirt with this cute guy that has just walked in,' he whispered into the phone. And he hung up on Ruby leaving her to face the predicament all on her own.

When still nothing surfaced after a good hour, she almost gave up. She daren't shut her eyes, fearing she would fall asleep into another nap. Ruby ran her eye over the employment searches online again. Nothing fresh had appeared in the last few weeks.

She practised the speech she would inevitably have to give in her head. 'Mum, I know this isn't ideal for either of us but do you think it would be okay if I came and stayed with you for a while? Not long. Just until I get myself on some financial footing.' A lump of sick threatened its way up her throat at the thought. She would somehow have to convince her mum to buy a fancy coffee machine. There was nowhere in town that did a decent espresso and her mum probably still chugged back that instant granulated stuff. Ruby shuddered at the thought.

No, she couldn't do it. She had to make this work. And not just because of the coffee. It was symbolic. It was going backwards. It was remaining a victim to circumstance and not breaking free like Cooper wanted her to do.

She heard his voice in her heard. 'Tell people what they want to hear.'

Ruby sought out Sally who was hidden away in her office, poring over files. Surprised to see Ruby, she shook her head a few times. As if she had been far away and forgotten that she was at work.

Ruby boldly stood at the edge of her desk and didn't sit down. She cleared her throat and lowered her chin. 'I'll be honest. I need a bit more time to get any solid information about this. As you can appreciate, it's not an easy task and finding missing people, especially if they don't want to be found can be difficult and near impossible. But I can let you know at this stage that Lucy is totally fine.' Ruby didn't know that but she guessed that the likelihood of him running into any real trouble was slim. And really only happened in the movies. It was most likely that he hooked up with some random and was stuck in a little love bubble that he didn't want to come out of. Or lost his phone after a big night out and needed some sleep. A man as beautiful as he surely had a social life to match.

'I see,' Sally said tersely. Ruby got the sense that no matter what she did she would never impress her.

'And...' just as Ruby was about to give some more platitudes and generalities, her vision blurred and the scene in front of her bounced back and forth a little, like it was trying to focus. What looked like a tunnel of light stretched out before her and at the end of it she saw a picture. In the picture was Sally, surrounded by white but looking far more dishevelled than Ruby could have imagined her. It almost took her a while to realise that it was indeed Sally. Her face was Rubenesque and blushed and she was in bed. It took a few seconds but Ruby realised what she was seeing: Sally was in a hospital bed.

'Yes?' Sally said impatiently, drawing Ruby back to the real world and away from the vision.

Was Sally sick? Ruby wondered to herself. It could explain the temperament and the impatience to get things done in a hurry. Maybe she didn't have much time left. This made Ruby's heartache a little. Even though Sally had shown no warmth to her and they may never get along, Ruby was awash with empathy and almost felt compelled to reach out and hug her. It was almost how she felt that night in the emergency room. But had the sense not to because this could have spelt an end to her job faster than anything else!

'Oh, I thought I almost had a vision then but it didn't quite come through clearly. Sorry. I'll let you know when it does.' Maybe Sally didn't even know she was sick. And far be it for Ruby to be the one to have to break the news. That's what doctors were for.

'You know,' Sally said conspiratorially, 'after I told both the investors the other day that we wouldn't be going with them— which I still think is ludicrous by the way, whatever is Walker thinking— I had this crazy and paranoid thought. *Could one of them be so upset with us that they have done something to Lucy?* The opportunity was big enough that it certainly would be motive to seek revenge on us somehow. If all goes to plan, they will be missing out on an absolute...' She paused and looked around even though it was just the two of them. She leaned her head forward towards Ruby and whispered, 'arseload of money.' The affected crassness shocked Ruby.

But it didn't slow Sally down. 'And Lucy has a lot of inside information. Far more than most people at his level would. Let me tell you that. He really does deserve the promotion he keeps pestering me about. I'm an idiot for not giving it to him sooner.'

Ruby pondered it and thought that she could be right about the investors. Sally was highly intelligent, which made her great at her job and what she lacked in people skills and social nuances she more than made up for in her shrewdness in business and hyperattention to detail.

'Ooh, look who's the psychic now!' Ruby attempted a joke which did not land well with Sally.

'I'm not psychic at all. I don't even believe in them, frankly.' She dismissed Ruby and let her eyes drop and continue to scan the files in front of her. With a second thought, she looked up and said, 'no offence.'

But Ruby wasn't offended, until recently she felt the same way. In fact, she was grateful for Sally. What she had suggested, although very macabre, could very much have some basis to it and she decided she needed to follow that pathway. It certainly couldn't hurt. 'Right, well I will leave you to it Sally and I'll report back the second I get anything further.'

'Be sure you do,' she said absently without looking at Ruby.

As Ruby mulled over what Sally had said in her office, she knew she was dancing around something. Even her own intuition, pre-psychic days would have told her the same. The wobble in Sally's voice and certainty of her accusation led Ruby to believe that Sally was onto something with the investors. Which was confirmed by the ease in which she handed over the investor files containing a lot of delicate information that would, ordinarily, be way above Ruby's pay grade.

Plopping down onto the boardroom floor, she scanned through each file with no real intention of reading it until she found what she was looking for: the address of each investor. Jotting them down in her phone, she took a deep breath and left the office, without a concrete plan or letting anyone know. All she knew was that she had to work out some way to help find Lucy. He was important to Sally and Walker and was quickly becoming important to Ruby.

It took her barely any time at all to walk to the first investor's office. Upon arrival, she reread the address in her phone several times. What she was presented with was in no way a match for the dowdy man that came to the office purporting to have millions of dollars on hand ready to throw at Crichton Enterprises' next big thing: ClairTech.

The shabby office's facade was lined with outdated wooden panelling which spoke more of a downtown dry cleaners than of a swanky financier type. Ruby shrugged to herself. Perhaps the new rich was to downplay it as much as possible. How would she know? She's never been rich. It's probably a security tactic. She pressed her face up to the window, shielding the light with her hand. Inside, she saw one bare desk and a tipped over rubbish bin. Not exactly the scene of a thriving business.

Ruby knocked on the door to no response. But with a determination that was quickly becoming a new part of her— and that she would happily admit— is a side of her that she liked, she knocked again. This time, in cadence with her knocking, a small dog barked alongside her. The Jack Russell, with a pointy caramel coloured snout and barely any legs, cocked its head at her so jauntily that Ruby thought it might keep going and twist around, like the hand on a clock face.

Looking at the dog, she knocked again three times. The dog barked three times in unison. 'Ha, ya little weirdo,' Ruby chuckled at it. 'Where's your owner then? Is this your office?' Ruby bent down and let it sniff her hand. It licked her offered hand and then lifted its eyes to hers. 'You're barking up the wrong tree,' the dog said to her. In a perfectly audible and reasonable human voice.

'Did you just talk?' Ruby retracted her hand quickly and looked around her, searching for anything that would explain the encounter. A person with a remote control. A hidden camera. A bunch of kids laughing at her. But there was nothing and not one other person was interested in her as they went about their daily business of walking quickly to whatever appointment they were late for. Or trying desperately to calm two quarrelling kids so they could get three minutes of peace for once.

The dog yipped to get Ruby's attention. 'You're barking up the wrong tree.'

Noticing that it hadn't been around since the funeral, she almost missed the soft voice that used to tell her what to do. She wished it would guide her now or, at the very least, tell her what to do about the awkward Walker-in-love-with-her situation.

Ruby took one last look at the abandoned office and decided to visit the next investor, which she hoped would have more luck and less talking animals. Looking down to the foot-path, the dog had already disappeared and Ruby shook her head. If this is what psychic life was about, how could she stop herself from looking like an insane person to the rest of the world?

The second investor's office turned out to be a two-storey mansion at the edge of the city. It belonged to the owner of the company who she had not met and who probably was never involved in any of the meetings the company took. Ruby pondered what it would be like to be one of those guys who just sent out people on their behalf to do the grunt work, whilst they stayed at home racking up the dollars for doing nothing but ordering people around. A part of it was mega appealing.

The tram ride there ate away the last of her emergency coins, so she spent the entire trip convincing herself that this had to be worth it and questioned not only her sanity, since she thought dogs were talking to her but why she was even doing this to begin with. It wasn't really her job. Yes, she desperately wanted to find

Lucy, hopefully, safe and well and in the arms of a handsome young man. But really, all she had to do was sit in the office and throw out a few buzzwords to earn her keep.

Because it's the right thing to do, she heard her inner voice say to her when she questioned herself. Ruby had never really been one for following the right, altruistic thing to do. Through her eyes, it was all about fixing herself and her life and once she had that side of things cornered, only then would she be in a position to help others. But the thing with that method was that she was in her early thirties and she wasn't even close to coming to an even keel and time was fast slipping away from her. Or so she felt.

After walking all the way up a paved driveway which took longer to traverse than watching an episode of her favourite show and a stronger incline than any treadmill could reach, she arrived at the gates of an enormous house, sweating and panting. Whilst waiting for her breathing to return to normal and the flush drop from her cheeks, she scanned the expansive garden that separated the house from her.

The grass was so green that it reminded her of jelly and the lavish palm trees that lined the edges clacked together in the gentle breeze. It could have been mistaken for a holiday resort.

'Fuck, maybe I really did get it wrong with the investors. We could have been having staff parties in this place! I bet there's a pool here. There has to be a pool,' she muttered to herself.

Ruby pressed the intercom button with her knuckle, sneakily trying to dab away the sweat on her top lip before the camera turned on. The intercom buzzed and offensive noise.

'Uh, hi. I'm from...' she paused and cleared her throat. '...Crichton Enterpris—' The gate buzzed open with another aggressive sound.

Purposefully and trying to ignore the glorious garden, Ruby walked up to the front double door and waited for it to open, which it did before she could even take a full breath.

'Well, well, well...' A smarmy voice that matched an equally smarmy face greeted her at the door. A weathered man dressed in a light blue polo top and khaki shorts stood with his chest and guts puffing out towards her.

Ruby felt sick all over as she realised who she was face to face with. 'You!'

'I knew you wanted me. Tracked me down, huh?'

Hot saliva rose from her throat as she found herself staring at Herman, her bookstore attacker. 'You're one of Crichton's potential investors?' Ruby could not believe it. But could now see exactly why her little voice suggested that the company didn't go with either of them. One was potentially broke and one was a bona fide slimy creep.

'Come to finish what we started, babe? I hope I didn't cause too much trouble with you losing your job. Seems that you've landed on your feet nonetheless.' Herman didn't take his eyes off her as he lifted his squat, perspiring glass of beer to his mouth and sipped noisily. Ruby caught a waft of the wheaty scent as he did so and it made her want to retch.

Ruby remembered the feeling of being trapped by him and looked around her towards the exit of the open gate, the other side of the charming garden. The man didn't deserve such a nice garden.

'I am absolutely not interested in anything you have to offer me,' Ruby said curtly.

'And yet—' Herman bobbled his head haughtily '—here you are!'

'I'm here on business only.' Ruby floundered. She really should have planned this more thoroughly because she was not managing to come up with anything useful to say to him and her psychic affinity was not kicking in fast enough. *Come on, you stupid gift. What is the point of you if you don't show up when I need you?* Red anger and embarrassment flushed her face.

Clearing her throat, she said 'I'm just apologising on behalf of Crichton Enterprises because we did not accept your investment offer and we hope this does not tarnish any future dealings.' Ruby slipped into a professional, robotic mode and hoped like heck that Sally had already informed him of their decision.

'I must say, it came as a surprise. Never really had anyone turn my money down before. I even offered a little extra. I could have stood to make an absolute bullock's load of money on that product you guys are working on there. It's gonna be a huge deal. Especially in the hands of someone like me, eh,' he winked at Ruby and mock saluted her with his drink.

It felt like tiny geckos were crawling over her entire body, their slimy sucky cups for hands pulling and threading at her skin, from her ankles all the way up her spine and over her scalp. She shivered and yearned to hop into a blasting hot shower. No words came.

'Oh well, next time eh.' Herman went to shut the door on Ruby but hesitated. 'Unless you want to...' he gestured inside.

Ruby was disgusted at herself for actually considering it, even for a moment. Not for any reason other than to find out more to help her track down Lucy. There had to be a safer way to find out if Herman had anything to do with Lucy's disappearance then to faux seduce the worm. The trauma would just not be worth it. 'Good day,' Ruby said and turned on her heel.

'Your loss bitch,' Herman slammed the door with gusto.

Ruby barely made it two feet across the superbly manicured lawn before she ducked behind one of the palms trees, a boiling rage pushing her on to uncover the trash that this man really was. The anger locked up her jaw and she rubbed her temples vigorously. Again, the ground vibrated around her and the tree she was leaning on started to wobble. The almost familiar roaring sound wound around her head and she knew what was coming. With little warning, her vision turned blurry and at the end of a mirrored tunnel, there stood Herman with a sweaty, self-righteous face. He sneered to Ruby as he said 'this is not the last time we'll be seeing each other, bitch.'

Ruby clawed at her own face, desperately trying to rid her mind of the vision and control it but she couldn't. The visions had their own timeline, she waited with alarm as she watched Herman laughing until he almost choked at the end of the passageway. Being psychic was starting to have its downside.

After what felt like an eternity but thirty seconds all at once, the vision abruptly ended and her eyesight blinked back to the luscious garden around her. She spat the sour taste out of her mouth straight into his erect agapanthus that stood like purple soldiers to attention.

With it, she spat out the unpleasant energy of him.

Waiting for the front gates to fully close, she continued to hide behind the palm tree, so Herman assumed that Ruby had long gone. With their closing, came safety but also came more danger.

Quickly, with her breath in her throat, Ruby sidestepped her way past the front door, half expecting it to swing open at any moment, and down the side of the house. She was right—there was a pool around the back just like she suspected there would be, she could just catch a glimpse of a corner of reflective blue water. It was enticing, she couldn't lie. Her skin begged her to jump in and wash away her troubles and her newfound mission and pathway. What she wouldn't give to escape from her predicament for even just five minutes. Like a total brain reset so she could start afresh. Yearning for the azure cool water and its relief there was also an underlying familiar twinge. She knew the feeling so well by now. It was such a default feeling that she didn't even know it was automatically running until now. Until she had developed the recent modicum of self-awareness. It was her victim mentality that was floating about beneath the surface. For so long it had been running her, like it was in charge of the way she thought and lived and not the other way around. Ruby didn't know exactly how not to revert to her victim temperament but she knew that she definitely wanted to.

Scanning the side of the house, she searched for a way to get in. At the front, she noticed four windows – there were four big rooms, two downstairs and two upstairs. And, she devised, that by the cube shape of the house, the configuration would be mirrored at the back, with a kitchen somewhere on the ground floor.

After making sure there were no pets lazing around the backyard— real or hallucinatory— she made her way to the back door which, she could see through the many panes of clear glass, lead straight into a wide kitchen. There was really nowhere to hide with all that glass exposure, so she just went for it and caught the curved handle of one of the double doors in her hand. It turned with ease and she slid through, at first placing one high heel tentatively on the shiny marble tiles and then allowing the rest of her body to catch up.

The kitchen, as she expected, was flawless and spotless. A marble counter the size of two single bed mattresses lined up spread across the centre of the room. It held nothing except for a three-tiered brass fruit bowl that was so flush with fruit: bananas, passionfruit, apples and mangoes. Her mouth watered just looking at it. Although there was a definitive smell of greed and waste that hung about. To Ruby, it smelt like metal and old soap. And to Ruby, it made her gag.

There were other doors in the kitchen: one led off to the right of her, one the left and one larger one which she assumed led to the foyer where Herman had greeted her from.

Now would be a handy time for that infamous psychic skill to kick in, she admonished herself, as she looked from door to door to decide which one to risk first. In the end, she opted for the door on the left, deciding that it might be safer than heading straight out to the foyer which, she saw from when Herman opened the door, was an open-aired space that could be entirely viewed from a ridiculous curved staircase that led to the second floor.

Tiptoeing across the slippery marble, she held her breath and tried her luck with the door handle, which again was open. Stepping inside, it was darker than the kitchen. There was none of that natural light that had no doubt been architecturally designed to be enjoyed. Blinking her eyes, she waited for her sight to adjust. When it did, she found she was face to face with shelves and shelves that were filled and neatly organised. The top shelf was lined with cereal boxes of blue, white and red and the three shelves below held small boxes and all sizes of jars that contained almost everything that Ruby could think of. The bottom shelves contained wire racks of potatoes and onions and it looked like a supermarket or a doomsday prepper's bunker. She had made it to the walk-in pantry.

Tempted to pocket it some of the tiny jars of gourmet marmalade, she decided against it and turned to go back into the kitchen to check out the other rooms for a skerrick of clues about

Lucy's whereabouts. But before she could step out, she heard the fridge door being pulled open. The familiar slurp of the suction breaking apart and the clink of a beer bottle told her that Herman was merely steps away.

She shrank back into the pantry, pressing her backside into the jam shelf behind her. The pantry door was still ajar and she hoped that Herman wouldn't notice it. With her heart racing, she held her breath and waited for Herman to leave so she could continue her exploration.

After a while, Ruby was sure the coast was clear as the fridge had been shut and there were no stirrings to be heard. But as she stuck her head outside the pantry, it seemed that she was wrong.

There sat Herman at the large wooden kitchen table, sipping his beer and admiring his shimmering pool. Quickly, Ruby tucked her head back in the pantry and panicked. How long could she stay in the pantry? He would have to retire to his bedroom eventually and then she could slip out. But what if he decided to cook dinner soon? Or reach for a packet of nuts to go with his beer.

But she didn't have much time to deliberate over her ill fate because her phone ensured that she was dumped right in the middle of danger for her. It bleeped piercingly and she recognised the sound as a bank notification. Her first lot of pay had finally been deposited into her account. She was as relieved as she was terrified.

'How long are you going to stay in there for?' Herman's voice came from his position lazily.

'Fuck.' Ruby had nothing.

'I saw you come in on the cameras, my dear.'

Ruby really felt like an amateur. Again, let down by her psychic skills. Sheepishly, she stuck her head out from the pantry and continued to tiptoe across the floor, although there was no longer any need to be subtle.

Herman turned, his torso and head all turning as one, in that stiff middle-aged way. 'I guess you really do owe me one now.' But his voice had lost conviction and he didn't bother with the wink. There was a more deflated sense to him and Ruby couldn't work out whether to be more terrified or relaxed.

Herman was such a disgusting creep that

Ruby let her imagination run away with her. There was no doubt that a man like that would keep someone innocent like Lucy locked up somewhere for his own amusement. Or, more likely, as revenge for not getting cut in on this mega-deal that Crichton Enterprises were apparently stirring up with the ClairTech. Ruby wished she'd been paying attention more to what the company does. What kind of product was ClairTech and why was it going to be so impressive? She knew they worked on a lot of sleep technology, which was interesting and had potential. But all they seemed to have released so far was a brain wave monitor an app for measuring how well you slept and what kind of brain wave activity your mind displayed when meditating. Whilst certainly fun, none of this was cutting edge. Now, if ClairTech was a flying car or holographic phone, then Ruby could understand the fuss.

But Herman was the type of guy that had never been told no, expect now by Ruby, twice. It must have been quite the blow to his ego, this younger woman turning up and blocking his advances to getting what he wanted. 'Well, there's my altruism for the year,' Ruby thought drily. And it just made her despise Herman even more.

Not wanting to risk it, with a few steps to go to cross the kitchen and make it to the double glass doors, she ran towards them. Her wrist burned as it twisted beneath her and her body weight crashed against the glass panes of the doors. The handle didn't move. The door was locked.

Shaking her sore wrist, she turned back to Herman. He held up his mobile to her and waved it side to side. 'Smart locking, silly. One of the perks of being filthy rich.'

Ruby pressed her back into the doors and scanned the kitchen again, weighing up her options. She could try to make a run for it through the foyer and out the front doors but if he had locked the back door, he had definitely locked the front door.

A sinking realisation hit her and she rubbed her tummy, hoping to rub it away, making it not real. No one knew she was here. No one knew that she was in pursuit of information about Lucy and no one would bother to come here looking for her. And the way that Herman was looking at her, suggested she was about to get murdered or violated in ways that she couldn't bear to think about. His bottom lip was sinking out to the side of his mouth and his eyes held a glassy look that made Ruby think of a dolphin's back.

'It looks like it's just us. Why don't you take a seat?' he said flatly. And kicked out the seat next to him. The solid oak chair legs scraped across the marble and let off a squeal.

Ruby hesitated and remained standing. Given the chance, she would run as fast as she could to get away from this creep. But, she knew, even if she did it would not solve the problem. The problem being Lucy. What hit Ruby was that now that she had enough money to back pay the rent and even pay some in advance— as well as all her overdue bills with enough left over to spend at Gloria's Spirit— was that she was still dying to find Lucy. Something inherently within her, rising up, that had nothing to do with her abilities or her loyalty to the company or her potential crush on Walker, beckoned her to make sure Lucy was safe and sound.

'Fine, don't sit down then.' Herman floppily waved his hand over the table in front of him. Tiredly, he hung his head for a few seconds before bobbing it up and struggled to look at her. It was only a few moments in time but the signs were there. It was then that Ruby realised that he was a bit drunk. Again, Ruby wasn't sure whether this increased or decreased her danger. Like almost everything when it came to Herman. For such a predictable middle-aged rich guy, he sure was erratic.

'Listen, Mr...' she paused waiting for him to help her fill out the formality. He didn't, he just kept watching her with heavy lids. 'Okay, Herman. I am sorry that it appears as though I am trespassing on your beautiful home,' she swept her arm around the kitchen, putting on an act of being impressed with the overt wealth on display. But the truth was, she was now more repulsed by it than ever. Almost as much as she was repulsed by his swollen, fat fingers that drummed on the table. They were so corpulent that she felt an urge to prick them with a pin to let their fatty sausage juice run out.

'It's jussa home,' Herman said to no one.

'Right. Well. No. It's not. It's a symbol. Of the kind of person you are and the status that you, no doubt, have earned.' With nothing to lose, Ruby thought nothing of blowing some smoke up his arse. 'It could be the other way round. I live in a real sorry apartment where I can literally reach a broom across from my couch to turn the oven off. And I'm ridiculously late on the rent and probably have an eviction notice waiting for me at home right now.'

'Hmph,' Herman found slight amusement in this. Ruby felt a small bit of triumphant in her comedic value. It was clearly slackening his defences.

'In fact, I've never seen a house so stunning. Would you be so kind as to give me a tour? I have a real interest in interior design, you see.' Ruby pulled out all the stops, tucking a bit of her wig behind her ears and flashing the broadest smile.

Herman was as simple in his desires as he was his pretence and he leapt up before Ruby even finished the sentence. 'Yes, yes! Let's tour this great palace. M'lady?' He offered her an elbow in a great show of melodrama. She took it graciously, all the while her insides boiling like a pot of gluggy pasta.

'I certainly don't need to show you the pantry. You've got that one covered,' he roared at his own joke and Ruby felt his gait go wobbly under her elbow. Technically, she could have shoved him hard in that moment but she wanted a legitimate way to snoop around the house as there is no way she'd be able to come back. If she ever made it out.

Ruby thought about how proud Cooper would have been to see her amateur acting performance then and there. Under the guise of being utterly absorbed in the nasty wallpaper, Ruby ran the tips of her fingers across it and asked as many legitimate sounding questions as she could. Sadly, nothing psychic was presenting itself and the act was draining her hope and her energy.

After no trace of Lucy, extrasensory or otherwise— in fact no trace of anyone in the house— Ruby felt despair as Herman walked her up the colossal staircase and pushed open the master bedroom door with one hand.

'And now, the room we've all been waiting for... drumroll please!'

'Oh, that's okay. Actually, I've just realised that I'm super late for my AA meeting and I really need to get going. If I'm not there on time, a whole bunch of angry alcoholics are going to come looking for me.'

'Pfft. Alcoholics. Most useless mob going,' he ironically slurred at her, standing a little too close to her and balancing on the balls of his feet. She wondered if she were to push him, would he fall over? A man of that confidence and wealth would likely just strike her across the face. It was clear from the bookstore interaction and locking the doors on her, that he already thought he could take what he wanted.

'One day at a time,' Ruby tried to banter cheerfully, fearful that once he got her into the master bedroom it would be harder to escape his vileness. *Or he could just pass out?* She thought to herself. But it wasn't a risk she was willing to take. She could already imagine how she would be victim-blamed for being in his house, let alone his bedroom in the first place. In the eyes of all who love to condemn, she didn't have a leg to stand on.

Ruby started scratching around her hairline, a half-formed plan revealing itself. She wished she brought her handbag with her rather than just tucked her phone into her back pocket, so she could swipe it at his ugly, pulsating head. Her eyes darted around her, looking for any kind of weapon. A vase or a golf club. But there was nothing. Not even a shoe. For a stereotypical wealthy blob, Herman didn't live up to the convenient tropes that would help Ruby escape his evil.

Instead, she yanked off her beloved wig with two hands and hurled it into his face. Grabbing the wig to his face, Herman was disorientated enough to grabble with it for longer than a sober person would and Ruby sought her break. There was a small gap between him and the staircase, so she elbowed him sideways as she thrust past. Feeling the banister rail underneath her hand, felt like freedom to her. All she had to do was make it down the stairs and out the front door.

Taking the cream carpeted stairs one at a time, she was careful to keep her eye line steady so as not to trip. Successfully reaching the bottom, her shoes clacking on the light marble, she made a last-minute decision to scurry back to the kitchen, forgoing the front doors not wanting to waste another second when he could catch up to her.

As she entered the kitchen, she heard an almighty guttural scream followed by a thud behind her. But Ruby didn't want to find out what had happened or what was about to happen to her so she stormed through the kitchen, grabbing the brass bowl of fruit on her way. Fruit went everywhere and she watched as a dozen apples rolled away from one another like a Christmas star lit up from the centre. Accidentally squishing a kiwi fruit beneath her shoe, she darted to the glass doors and brought the bowl down hard into one of the panes of glass. Ready to strike again she brought the bowl above her head but there was no need— the glass fell away easily, leaving an open space bordered by jagged shards. Carefully shielding her face, she hacked at the remaining glass creating enough room that she could slide sideways through, without lacerating her torso.

Suddenly, Ruby's ears were filled with the sound of a wounded bird. But upon realising it was just the house alarm shattering the air, she hastened her actions, fearing Herman was right behind her and any minute a damp heavy hand would clamp down on her. But as she ran across the front grass and the shrieking bird started to quieten, the hand never came.

Coming up against the closed front gate, she slipped the toes of one foot onto the wrought iron, which immediately slid straight off. As she crab walked over to the gate's pillar, she frantically searched for a release button but found nothing. The gate would not budge as she yanked it towards her and then pushed it away with all the strength she could summon.

Her face turned beetroot and a dribble of sweat slid into one eye. The pull of being a victim was glaring her in the face. She could have easily sunk down onto that lovely grass and cried. But she had already decided, somewhere within her, that she was going to live differently. Be a different person. One that didn't resort to her old habits of being a victim. When she realised that she hadn't been succumbing to the attractive call of victimhood, even just by making the decision to change, a new potency showed itself.

Clutching her wig cap off her clammy head, she wound it around her hand. The beige mesh fabric created a grip that she used to grab one of the forged spokes that lined the top and haul herself up. Even though her heels slid all over the place, she hurled herself over the electric iron gate, one leg at a time while the spokes jabbed into the flesh of her belly. On the road side, she hung from one hand and could feel the skin stretching across her armpit. She puffed and blew her hair out of her eyes and let go, falling to the ground beneath her. *What a day to wear heels,* she thought as ground's impact jarred all the way up through her legs. She crawled across the paved driveway until the jarring feeling had left her legs and then she took off in a hobbled run.

Despite the painful banging of her heart as she got away as fast as she could, she felt more relieved than ever. More than when the bank app notification dinged in her pocket, more than when Cooper denounced his grudge and welcomed her back into his sparkly energy and more than when she got the job with Crichton Enterprises. But she absolutely couldn't ignore the sadness that threatened to break through her eyes that she was no closer to finding Lucy.

Chapter 16

Chapter 16

The number of rosemary plants she bought was a little over the top. After she had a chain lock installed, she lined up six in little ceramic pots against the small wall on the inside of her doorway. It was like she was greeted by a kerosene torch pathway in some ritualistic fire-walk. Additionally, she strung up bundles of fresh rosemary sprigs tied together with whatever she could find: leftover twine, ribbons from decorative boxes of chocolates and even tape. On the bedside table, she placed a small jar of rosemary in water and sprinkled any discarded leaves across the base of her bedroom window.

'This is ridiculous,' she said to herself out loud. 'But if I'm doing it, I'm doing it,' and sniffed the air. The shop owner's advice might have suddenly turned into the start of a hoarding disorder but at least it smelt like a Sunday roast inside her cosy apartment.

Next up she heaped the salt in a thick line across the front of her doorway. The neighbour that lived above her looked at her like she needed a long lie down but it didn't deter Ruby. For she was intent on being as protected as she possibly could, especially after what went down at Herman's house.

Nausea hit Ruby's throat and stomach when she thought about Herman coming after her and how she got away, leaving a mess of smashed glass that Herman would find and no doubt being extremely angry about. And she was annoyed that she had to forego her precious wig. She made a mental note to call Cooper and see if he could get her another one. And relay the whole wretched story of Herman's house, of course.

Ruby thought about what Cooper would suggest doing about Lucy. She wasn't sure that 'tell people what they want to hear,' would be useful in this situation and Ruby realised that she was way over her head. This wasn't what she planned. It certainly wasn't in her— albeit elusive and unconventional— job description. She just wanted a job and now she had ended up in a dangerous position. But she was re-minded of the pay that came through and how she effortlessly paid off her owed rent as soon as she got home and how good it felt not to be under the constant terror of being kicked out. And, if she worked a bit more with Crichton En-terprises, she could start saving a deposit for a bank loan. And with that bank loan she could start her own bookstore. The dream unlocked.

Ruby sighed at the thought of being back in her natural habitat of books, smelling their sweetness and pretending she could hear them tell her of the words contained within. There would be no slimeball customers like Herman. Cooper could work there— if he wanted to— and every weekend he could use it for his the-atre productions. There could be themed cocktail nights that she could tie in with books: like *The Great Gatsby* night or *The Big Sleep*. Making a mental note, she considered asking Ana next time she was in Cynthia's what she thought about a potential collaboration. Everything felt like it was meant to be.

The sense of bliss and peace swam through her chest and refreshingly swallowed her. Light on her feet, she waltzed around the house inhaling the heady rosemary, giddy with the potential of a dream she'd held since she was a child. Smiling to herself in the bathroom mirror, she said 'finally! Finally, it's all working out for you Ruby.' She thought she saw a tear wobble in her eye but before she could be sure the bathroom mirror faded to black, like the end of a movie. In place of her reflection was a polished, endless surface. Lifting her hand, she cautiously touched it with two fingerpads but, to her surprise, it felt cool just like her ordinary bathroom mirror. It was so shiny that Ruby expected it to squeak when she touched it. As she peered at it, it trembled, like someone was adjusting it in the light, back and forth, back and forth.

Ruby was mesmerised and thought she could see herself and her future inside the surface. But the image was so weak that she couldn't be sure she was seeing anything except a reflection of the bathroom bulb.

I know what this is. It's the scrying mirror! She thought. *Of course.* Remembering back to her goods bought from Gloria's Spirit, she kicked herself for not using it sooner. Thankfully, her sixth sense was on her side to remind her. For once.

She crunched through some rogue salt in the kitchen and found the overlooked paper bag.

Reaching into the bag, she plucked out the handled scrying mirror and settled on the couch and waited. It was hard to look into the slab without being self-critical. Ruby wanted to pick apart the way her nose was too skinny in the middle, which made it seem far too long for her face. Or how her cheek pads sunk forward too much. Maybe some cheek fillers were in order? *No, you must save to get your own book shop*, she chided herself. *Who cares what you look like?* But like everything, she had an answer for that too. *Err, me? And potential suitors?* But in the end, she rolled her eyes at herself too distracted to continue to argue with her own conscience.

After sitting with the scrying mirror for a long time, alternating with the lights on and off, nothing leapt at her from it. There was nothing there for her except the sound of her inner critic, which even she was getting bored of.

Sneaking a peek back at the bathroom mirror, she was disappointed to see that it had returned to normal and reflected the creamy tiles of her bathroom. What was it trying to tell her that she missed?

Yawning, she rationalised that it had probably not been trying to tell her anything and she was just exhausted from a traumatic day. Placing the scrying mirror on the bedside table, she snuck in between the sheets and placed them over her head. Astonishingly, Ruby instantly fell into one of the deepest sleeps she'd ever had.

Chapter 17

Chapter 17

Awaking groggy and feeling thick in the face, Ruby let the hot water of the shower assault her. She washed her hair several times, hoping she would find a way to style it elegantly to compensate for the missing wig.

To make herself feel better, she still dressed in head to toe black, with a sleeveless turtle-neck, ankle-length pencil skirt and boots that ended just below the ankle but were covered in lines of silver studs. Lucy, if he were in the office, would have been so proud of her shoe choice, especially as the soles of her feet were bruised from landing on them the day before.

The thought made Ruby sigh with despondency. She hoped that he would just turn up like nothing had happened and be perched at his desk, raising one sharply drawn eyebrow at her, sporting a new nose or lip ring.

Treating herself, Ruby took a cab to work, promising herself it was just this once and she wouldn't blow all her money right away. Besides, she was already an hour late because she was trying to mangle her hair into something presentable.

Walker had been avoiding her, it was obvious. Other than the reveal that Lucy had gone missing, he wouldn't look her in the eye or interact with her. When she tried to greet him for the day he pretended that he didn't hear her, instead just doodling on a notepad in front of him on his desk. And when she was in the staff kitchen pouring herself a coffee, she swore she felt and smelt him come to the door and turn around once he saw she was in there. But she could have been mistaken because there was no sign of him when she toddled back to her makeshift office with her lukewarm mug of black coffee.

In a way, Ruby was relieved. It was much easier that he was avoiding her than trying to have to figure out how to navigate her boss having a crush on her when she was still trying to help find Lucy and keep her job. Ruby crossed her fingers together, pressing them hard until her skin turned white. 'Please don't let me get fired because Walker likes me, please,' she silently begged the air.

Before going to her own office, she took a lap around the other side of the office. Disappointment hit her tummy when she saw that Lucy's desk was empty and left the way she last saw it.

'Ruby!' Sally shrieked at her from her office. She came bustling out, her stockinged feet shoeless again. Ruby could hear the stiffness of her suit jacket rubbing against itself as she leapt out of her office and cowered, afraid she'd done something wrong. But Sally swept Ruby up in her arms and held her tightly. Ruby could feel Sally's balled fists pressing firmly into her back. Into her ear, she said loudly, 'oh thank goodness. We thought they got you too!'

Ruby awkwardly tittered once Sally finally

let her go. Her reaction had thrown her. 'No, no I'm fine. Well. They haven't got me.' Ruby smiled weakly and thought Sally was trying to hold back tears. But assured herself that it must be her imagination.

'My... you do look different. Different hair?' Sally said, her eyes belying her truth.

Ruby self consciously touched her hair, regretting the deep side part she attempted. 'Yeah, normally I wear a wig but...' she stopped not knowing how to finish the sentence.

'Yes, yes. So that's your natural hair then?' Sally came closer and picked up a section of hair between her fingers and looked at it. Ruby swore it was disdainfully but it could easily have been curiosity.

'Ha, yeah. Not quite as glam, I know!'

'No, it's lovely. It's a lovely colour. I wasn't expecting such a rich burgundy underneath.'

'Oh. You knew it was a wig?'

'Mm hmm,' Sally look caught out.

Of course they knew it was a wig. It was, after all, so very obviously a wig. Ruby felt silly for wearing something so silly the entire time.

'I was thinking I would go back to my natural

colour a bit more. There's really no need for me to be sporting a wig. I'm not in disguise after all.' Ruby laughed at her own joke but Sally returned to her customary poker face and it made Ruby shut down, quickly. Sally had a unique way of making situations feel awkward.

'I think you're very lovely to look at,' Sally said unceremoniously as if she had commented on the weather. Ruby was taken aback by the compliment. Unsure if she meant it, she was still touched.

'Anyway. Truly, I'm glad you're alright. I was so worried when I couldn't find you yesterday and I didn't have your phone number,' she continued.

'Oh, I'm so sorry. I took off yesterday afternoon on... a psychic lead. I should have told someone, that's my fault.'

'No need to apologise, Ruby. I'm pleased that you are okay. It's bad enough that someone I love has gone missing, let alone you too.'

Love? She loved Lucy? Ruby was surprised that a woman like that who was so bound up, so in control of every twitch of her face, was capable of love and even more capable of declaring it so. And did she truly care about Ruby, too? She didn't have to be a psychic to know that this meant one of two things: that Sally knew something more than she let on and that Lucy truly was in deep danger. Or Sally was so much more of a soft-hearted woman than she let on. And Ruby didn't know which was more disconcerting to be honest.

'So no word from Lucy yet?' Ruby asked optimistically.

'None.' Sally looked forlornly at his empty desk.

Tell them what they want to hear, Ruby thought. 'I have a really good feeling that he will turn up soon enough and that he is safe and well.'

Sally instantly brightened. 'You really feel that?'

'I do indeed,' Ruby smiled directly at her. 'But I thought you didn't believe in psychics,' Ruby winked at her.

'Well, I don't. I didn't. I don't know. All I know is that I need all the hope I can get right now. Anyway, I best get back to it. Let me know if you have any more "feelings" about Lucy.'

'Straight away. I promise.' Ruby sauntered off to her place in the boardroom but barely made it in before Sally rushed in, her mauve pointy shoes back in place, ensuring he was a full foot taller than Ruby. Her maternal air had vanished and Ruby thought she had imagined the woman that had held her against her bosom.

'Where is your wig, Ruby?' Sally asked with a strange look.

'About that... Why do you ask?' Ruby said preparing herself to reveal to Sally how she probably broke the company policy against privacy and confronted their investors. *Good luck ever getting money to get ClairTech off the ground*, she thought to herself.

'Oh... nothing. I just... thought maybe you could bring it in tomorrow and I try it on? See if it's a look I want to adopt.'

Ruby chuckled with disbelief. 'But you have gorgeous hair... why...' And then Ruby remembered the hospital vision that she had of Sally not so long ago. She couldn't help but imagine Sally withering away in a hospital bed or curled up on a chair enduring the torment of chemo treatments and losing her golden hair. Sally's more maternal edge and willingness to slowly divulge her emotions suddenly made more sense.

Ruby took a deep breath and softened in every area of her body. She moulded her face into one she hoped was sympathetic and caring. Her heart broke a little for her now at this moment. 'Listen, normally I would have no hesitation in letting you try it. But there's something I have to tell you.'

'Go on,' Sally said, her voice becoming harder. She fiddled with the back of her small gold earring as she tilted her head to one side.

'This is not easy to say. And I want you to know that I truly have the best interests at heart. I just wanted to find Lucy you see.'

'Do I need to sit down for this?'

'By all means,' Ruby pointed to a chair and took up her own.

'Well get on with it, I haven't got all my life,' Sally snapped and it became further entrenched that Sally felt the time pressure of a looming fatal disease.

'I know I shouldn't have done this. I know

how wrong it is and how bad it looks for the company. But something you said yesterday really made me believe I was on the right pathway.'

'Ruby, what did you do?'

'I stole the investor files and went to confront them,' Ruby squeezed her eyes shut, awaiting Sally's lambasting. Prying one eye open, she looked at Sally who was staring straight ahead at her with no expression.

'And?'

'Nothing. Well, not nothing. Andy's company is likely going broke from the state of his abandoned office. So I really don't know how they were going to fund us. And Herman? From the second investor's office? Well...' Ruby paused for effect, making sure Sally was listening. 'He is the biggest piece of shit that has ever existed.'

'Ain't that the truth,' Sally rolled her eyes at the thought of him.

'Anyway, I snuck into Herman's house...'

'Wait. What? You broke into his house?' Sally was incredulous.

'I know. I know! But I just feel compelled to find Lucy, you see. I've grown very fond of him.'

'I do understand that.' Sally tightly nodded for Ruby to proceed.

'Long story short, to defend myself I threw my wig at him, like some terrible eighties slapstick movie and now it's still at his house. And, worst of all, there's absolutely zero sign of Lucy.'

Sally sat in silence drawn-out enough to build cities in. Which gave Ruby enough time to plan out a lengthy and emotional apology in her head.

'I see,' she finally said.

'I'm sorry, I...' But she held up a hand which prompted Ruby to stop in her tracks.

'There's no need. Really. I just have to... sort some things out,' and she rushed out of the boardroom so fast that some papers on Ruby's desk flapped up and down in protest.

Ruby fished out her phone and made a long-overdue call. But she hit a wall when she heard the familiar voicemail greeting. 'Hey, it's Cooper. I probably won't check this so don't leave a message.' She ignored his instructions as she often did.

'Edward. It's me. Some wild shit has gone down. First of all, this guy Lucy, I know— a guy with the name Lucy, so modern, so art, we love to hear it. Anyway, you'd love him, he's gorgeous and sassy and gay like you. And you love gays! Wink, wink. Anyhoo, he's gone missing. So very TV, right? Well like the impulsive idiot that I am, I thought I could play Miss Detective Psychic Sleuth and have things work out just like the movies—' cut off by the beep of the voicemail ending, she called back.

'... as I was saying, so I went to this investor's house who I thought might have kidnapped Lucy— I can't believe I am saying these things out loud. And you'll never in a hot minute guess who the investor was? None other than Herman the piece of sausage sleaze. As if we didn't need any more reasons to hate him. Long story short, he tried to keep me captive in his house, but I threw my wig at him and escaped. It was a whole big thing. Call me back. Byeeee.'

Ruby sat panting at her desk. Reeling from how absurd her tale sounded and how fast she spat it out over the phone. She only looked up when there was a gentle rap on the door jam. A friendly looking lady with a short spiky hairdo and thick-framed glasses stood there.

'Hi love, sorry to bother you but you have a delivery.'

Ruby wasn't expecting anything and she certainly didn't expect the endearing lady to brandish a bouquet of flowers bigger than her torso from behind her back. The flowers spilled out over the clear vase they sat in. Orange lilies, mixed with purple irises and sprigs of greenery. It was as bold as Ruby's life choices and she absolutely loved it. Blushing, she carefully took the oversized bundle from the lady and thanked her profusely. 'Don't thank me, love. Just doing my job. Thank whoever sent them to you.'

Which prompted Ruby to search for the card. Nestled amongst the flowers was a small card the size of a credit card. Inside it read: *I'm finding it harder and harder to deny the way I feel about you.*

A thick lump worked its way up Ruby's throat. Her visions and suspicions about

Walker had been right. He had developed some kind of crush on her! On someone he barely knew, who he thought had short black hair and not the wavy, auburn mop that was truly her own. She had to set things straight with him, just have it out with him, be clear that it was inappropriate and that they could not progress.

But before she confronted him, she made sure that her hair had more volume by sliding her fingers along her scalp and shaking them at the roots. She reapplied a subtle pink gloss to her lips thanks to her phone camera and popped in a breath mint. By the time she had made it to her office, an army of ants had overtaken her intestines.

She lightly coughed to get his attention, which didn't work. 'Walker?'

He looked up at her, his usual cheery disposition all but drained from his being. 'What is it?' He pushed what he was reading out of his eye line and leant back in his chair, rubbing his temples before focusing on Ruby.

Tentatively, Ruby approached his desk.

'I'm not going to sit down. This won't take long.'

'Is it about Lucy?' Walker asked hopefully.

'No, I'm afraid not.'

'Then can it wait?'

Walker's abrupt tone put Ruby on edge. But she had to get this out. Make things clear from the start so there was no confusion. And if that made him act like this, then she could bear the brunt of it.

'I won't say that I haven't entertained this, haven't thought about the glorious potential of it but I need to be straight with you.'

'Spit it out please Ruby. I like you working here but I need you to hurry things up so I can focus on finding a new investor. Since we need one, stat.' he looked at her like it was her fault.

'I really like this job. I love it in fact. And not just because I need it. And I can't do anything to jeopardise that.'

'Glad to hear. We think we've made a sensible hire with you.'

A sensible hire? That did not sound like a very romantic way to flirt with someone you just sent flowers to.

'Right. Speaking of sensible, I don't think it would be very sensible for us to pursue something with one another. Even though the attraction is obviously there. It's just too risky. For both of our jobs.'

The silence was palpable. Ruby felt like she could pick it up and toss it out the window.

Walker's face crumpled into what looked like agony and Ruby was convinced he was going to cry, which she was not at all prepared for. But what she really wasn't prepared for was Walker bursting out into laughter.

'Oh, I do apologise Ruby. It's not funny... it's just...' and with that, he cracked up laughing again.

'Should I be insulted by this? Because I think it's the right thing to do. The flowers were nice and all...'

'Flowers?'

'Yeah, the lovely bouquet I just got. Which I assumed were from you given that...'

'Oh, Ruby. You are lovely but I definitely didn't send you flowers. I'm sorry if I have been overly friendly— it has genuinely come from a place of trying to make you feel welcome. I know that Sal hasn't exactly been warm.'

'Oh, God.' Ruby said as her face flushed the

same colour as her name. She lowered her head and placed her hands on her knees and took some deep exaggerated breaths.

'Are you okay?'

'Perfectly, fine,' she said, in between breaths. 'Just grappling with intense humiliation and possible job loss from an innocent mistake.'

'Look I'm flattered Ruby but the flowers weren't from me. I'm not surprised, though. I'm sure you're a catch. You look great without that darn wig, too. What made you think they were from me?'

'The vision,' Ruby said hesitantly.

'You had a vision about me? I guess I'm rather flattered.' He wiggled his tie appreciatively.

'Yeah, you were telling me in your office that you loved me. And I thought that you were developing some sort of infatuation with me.'

'I see. I can assure you that is not the case and this is nothing but a professional relationship. Perhaps your unique... gift...' it was the first time that Ruby had heard him use any derision in regards to what she did. '...is a little off.'

'It must have been. I'm so sorry. I'll leave you to finding a new investor. But sing out if you need my help!'

'Sure.'

Ruby slunk off back to her office, unable to shake the warmth from her cheeks. She was so shaken that her vision was so completely off base that she started to question every vision she'd had.

Pulling the whiteboard from the darkened corner of the boardroom and standing in front of it, she determinedly plucked the cap off the marker and began to write down each vision:

> *Walker saying "I love you" and crying over love lost, more than once*
> *Sally in hospital*
> *Herman saying he'd see her again*
> *Cooper's cousin*

Her hand hovered as she thought to write about the office fire. But deciding that was un-equivocally a coincidence, she promptly forgot about it. The same thing when she considered happening up Ana at the bar that night. Despite the pungent tequila smell and a feeling in her tummy, she didn't exactly have a vision.

How many of them had come true? She went through the list. The first one was a definite and humiliating no. One that she wouldn't forget in a hurry.

Sally in hospital— well there was no way to tell that yet as it seemed like a future prophecy. It was true, she could argue that she did see Herman again so soon after she thought she had left him. Then there was Cooper's cousin. She wasn't even sure that belonged in the same category, that was another kettle of fish alltogether. But what she was told was confirmed by Cooper so she had to take it as a win. That was a likely fifty per cent strike-rate with twenty five per cent hanging in the balance.

Ruby pondered over what she had written on the board and realised she was wasting time and felt stupid. The humiliation had made her question herself and worse, doubt her abilities, which she had been so blindly putting so much faith into. That is always a dangerous thing to be relying on something so new without proven results.

Ruby vowed to herself that she would no longer be solely relying on this mystical information that came to her. Instead using her logic and brain to help her see things through. Which she realised, as she stared at the board a little harder, had a much lower strike rate than her gifts, if she was brutally honest.

Ruby stood up and stretched her legs. Looking out the window, she watched the tiny people dart beneath the tall building. She wondered if any of them had the same problem. Surely there must be at least a few of them that also shared this gift, no doubt some with much stronger and all-pervasive senses. How did they know what information to trust and what to disregard? She missed the warm, comforting voice that had started all of this. If it could just pop out of thin air right now and tell her what the secret is to believing or listening to mystic guidance, then she would be able to avoid any future humiliation or getting it wrong.

Ruby checked her phone and noticed several missed calls from Cooper. But before she could call him back, the receptionist popped her fair head in. 'Uh, Ruby? Can you come out here please? There are some... police,' she whispered the word, '... here to see you.'

Ruby's stomach dropped. Herman! They were bound to arrest her for trespassing on his property. Was that something people went to jail for? Or would she have to pay a fine? It saddened Ruby that just as she was getting her finances together, they would be taken away from her. 'That's just how the universe works, I suppose,' she conceded quietly to herself.

'I'll be right there,' Ruby brightly told the receptionist. Whatever they thought, she was going to present confidently and maintain her innocence. Indeed, she was purely at Herman's on business. To follow up the investor meeting. That's all.

In the reception area, stood two police officers in uniform. One shorter lady, with a thick blonde plait and strong eyebrows smiled at her warmly. The other, about a foot taller, had brunette hair in a low bun and a thin face. She was nowhere near as warm, so Ruby turned her attention on the shorter police officer.

'I'm Ruby,' she swept out confidently and

offered her hand, which the shorter officer went to take but thought twice when she noticed the brunette ignore it.

'Ruby?'

'That's me! Need a little help solving a case? I'm a renowned corporate psychic you know.' Ruby winked at them but the foolishness was eating her up inside. But she figured she didn't have a lot to lose.

'Actually, can you confirm your whereabouts yesterday afternoon?'

'Certainly can. Mostly, I was at home. Why do you ask?'

'It's come to our attention that you were at the residence of a Mr Herman Shaslinger and that he tried to impede you from leaving his property. Can you verify this information?'

Ruby's face started to wobble. She was thrown. Was it a trick to getting her to confess that she snuck into his place, threw something at him and then smashed his door?

After some silence, whilst the police officers studied her face, the blonde poised with her pen hovering over her small notepad, the brunette office declared, 'we have CCTV footage of you inside the house ma'am.'

'Yes, it was me! But I didn't mean to. Tell Herman that I'll pay for his door to be replaced and that I'm so very sorry. I was just scared.'

'Ma'am, there's no need. He's under arrest for unlawfully detaining you. We just need you to come down to the station and verify a few things, is that possible right now?'

'Yes. I'll come right away! How did you know about me?'

'One of his house staff called in an emergency last night when they arrived for work. They found him lying at the bottom of the stairs in the foyer unconscious.'

Ruby's hand flew to her mouth and she couldn't help herself. 'Holy fuck! Oops, sorry. Am I allowed to swear? Of course I am, what am I talking about? You're the police, not a priest.'

'We appropriated his internal TV monitoring to determine the cause of his fall. Whether it was something untoward or just an accident. Considering the broken glass everywhere, we suspected a break-in. But the tapes just showed him locking you in whilst he drank with you.

And then him cornering you upstairs and you throwing your... ahem,' brunette cleared her throat and there was no hiding this time that she was thoroughly enjoying this, '...your wig at him. And then he tumbled down the stairs of his own accord. A terrible accident, where he lost his footing. It appeared as though he was very drunk, would you agree?'

'He was slurring his words.'

'He is... fine. If you were wondering?' The brunette said and Ruby swore she could see her eyes smile.

'Well, I'm not going to lie. I'm not terribly fussed at his state of wellbeing. I'll just grab my things and come with you now.'

Chapter 18

Chapter 18

Having cleared her name with the police, she went back to work, which had quickly become one of her favourite places to be. Ruby was relieved that she was in no real trouble and that Herman was going to be okay. Just a cut on his head, which hopefully meant that he wouldn't be messing with young women any time soon. Ruby secretly hoped that the fall had been strong enough to knock his head and bang his frontal lobe. She'd read about people becoming completely different from their ordinary selves just by hitting this area of the brain. But who knew? Dirtbags like Herman had run society for years, it's not as if one little incident would change their behaviour.

Knocking on Sally's door, she didn't wait for her to welcome her in. 'I just wanted you to know that the police did a thorough search of Herman's house and there was absolutely no sign of Lucy there. I'm sorry to report.'

'I know.' Sally was as brusque as ever.

'Oh. How do you know? Have you found him?'

But Sally remained quiet, she seemed to be mulling something over. But to Ruby, she was getting really tired of the way Sally treated her. She suspected it was some leftover humiliation from her interaction with Walker.

But she couldn't help herself and it all boiled up within her and she let Sally have it. 'I get that you don't necessarily like me and you don't believe in psychics so much. And that is totally okay. You don't have to, to appease me. But you have to treat me with some goddam respect. I know you're the boss and I know that I'm totally out of line here but I've had a heavy few days and everything I have done has been in aid of this place and helping to find

Lucy. Your coldness is not warranted.' Ruby's heart hammered at her chest and her cheeks flushed. She could already feel the sweat pooling at the back of her neck. She was not emotionally equipped to deal with how Sally was going to react to her outburst. She wished she had someone here for support. Cooper or Lucy. Or even the brunette officer who had grown to like her, eventually, and asked if she could book a private psychic reading.

The quiet was all too painful for Ruby to bear. Her eyesight bounced from the window to the floor to Sally who was cradling her head in her hands and taking long deep breaths.

Ruby didn't want to wait around for the wrath. 'I'm sorry that was inappropriate. I'm just going to go now.' But then Ruby heard something utterly unexpected and it nearly made her keel over.

Sally sniffed. It wasn't an angry sniff. It was a sad sniff. It was a snotty sniff. Sally was crying. Her head bobbled up and down.

'Oh Sally, are you okay?' Ruby rushed forward and unsure whether to comfort her or not, let her hand hover over the top of her glistening hair.

'I'm fine. Really,' Sally wiped her nose with the back of her hand. And then she cried harder than before. 'See? I'm fi—' She couldn't even finish the word "fine" because she howled through huge sobs.

'Oh shit, Sally. Fine isn't what this is,' Ruby said as she waved her hand in circles around Sally's face.

'It's all my fault,' she said through breathy sobs. 'All of this. It's. My. Fucking. Fault.'

Ruby couldn't help herself but she was loving the dishevelled manner of Sally as her hair came loose out of her alligator clip and globs of grey tears had fallen on her cream blouse. Her knuckles and her eyes were red raw and it delighted Ruby to see how beautifully human Sally was.

'It's not your fault. You can't be responsible for this,' Ruby said earnestly.

'You don't understand. It is my fault. All of this is my fault. Lucy missing, Herman messing around with you.'

Ruby lifted her hand off Sally's shoulder

ever so slowly and moved her body around to face her. 'What do you mean, Sally?'

Sally sniffed up some snot that was wildly cascading onto her upper lip and took a deep breath. 'I can't tell you. I want to. It's high time, but I can't. Not just yet. I made Lucy do some things which weren't exactly... ethical. And I know he aspired for a promotion for ages and he well deserves it. Especially now. I guess he felt it was implied that if he went through with this, he would be guaranteed that promotion.'

'What? What have you made him do?'

'He's been helping the company implant and install ClairTech. But I know that he is such a good guy that this would be weighing on his mind. And if the investors had nothing to do with this then he has run away from us. I guess he needed a break from feeling bad or wanted to feel safe in his own right. I just want him back.'

An untethered confusion whirled Ruby around and around. With it came a little bit of hope that they could still find Lucy. She didn't really understand the gravity of what Sally was saying but it didn't matter. She knew they could find Lucy, somehow.

But before she could suggest such, the walls started swaying and Ruby thought she could smell metal. But it wasn't metal, it was a distinct hospital smell. And the vision of Sally in hospital reappeared. This time in much clearer resolution and like Ruby was actually in the vision, not just standing at the end of it.

Sally was in a brightly lit hospital room, the curtains drawn back to allow a thick beam of sunshine in. The sun stretched through and touched everything in its path and left its mark at the foot of Sally's bed. There were several bouquets of flowers around the room which, combined with the sunlight, brought a cheeriness to the room. Ruby didn't want to look at Sally lying in the bed, fearing what she might be witnessing. But something beside the bed caught her eye. Between the bed and the window, lay a clear Perspex cradle. And in it was a tiny, red bundle asleep. Ruby looked to Sally who lay propped up in bed with a glowing face. She could see it better now. Sally wasn't sick, she'd just given birth. And she was so much younger, so much healthier, so much happier than Ruby could have ever imagined her. The joy that emanated from her entire being as she dipped her hand low to cup it over the baby's wrapped torso was unmistakable. The vision was beautiful and gratifying and caused a sharp intake of breath in Ruby.

'What is it, Ruby?' Sally asked as she was catapulted back out of the vision.

'I saw you! I saw you in hospital. This is the second time that I've had this vision and at first, I thought you were sick and I didn't want to tell you. Or admit that I knew in case you were keeping it private. But this vision was... beautiful. You had a baby!'

Sally's face dropped so fast that Ruby was concerned she was going to faint. Suddenly all her tears and snot had dried to her face and the redness was gone. In its place was a pale sheen which alarmed Ruby. It reminded her of Cooper's cousin's face in the casket.

'How did you know that?'

'Oh, it really happened? How delightful. I didn't know you had a child.'

'I don't have a child. How did you know that I gave birth?'

'I told you, I just saw it in a vision. There was sunshine streaming in through the window and three bunches of flowers along the side of the room. And you were just so happy.' Ruby smiled at the memory of the vision.

'Nobody knows about that. How can you know?'

'Because I'm psychic! Believe it or not.' Ruby announced it with glee. It felt good to say it out loud and claim it. There certainly was no going back now. It had tipped the number of visions that came true over to more than half and, to her, it was a clear sign that something special had occurred within her. But how could she be wrong about the vision about Walker? Maybe he was saying something else? Ruby wished she could summon up the vision again to get a little more clarity.

Sally dropped her chin and cracked her knuckles beneath her. 'I did have a son. I was so very young. I wasn't ready. I couldn't have done it. I'm a career woman and there's not much room in my life to compete with the passion I have for making a career come to life. I knew that then and I still know it today. So I had to give him to a home that had room for him in their lives as well as their hearts.' She paused and looked out the window.

'But he has always sat in my heart and I think about him every day. He's the same age as Lucy. I know it sounds silly but I consider Lucy to be a representation of the son that I had but chose not to raise. That's why he's so important to me. That's why him going missing is making me lose my centre. To be honest, it's made me question everything I know to be true. Maybe career isn't the be-all and end-all of my life? I don't regret giving up my child for adoption, I know that the was the best thing but I can't help but wonder... Anyway. It doesn't matter now. I just want Lucy back.'

Ruby was dumbstruck into silence. Her heart completely softened towards Sally. It suddenly made sense why she was so cagey and cold and why finding Lucy was turning her inside out. Armed with this new information it was hard not to see Sally in a new, positive light and have enormous affection for her.

Sally shifted uncomfortably in her seat. 'Nonetheless, this is all out of your paid role. You shouldn't have to hear me blab on about my problems. You're not here for that. I must admit though, you've definitely convinced me you have a gift. And I also must apologise for letting myself come undone so many times in your presence. It's very unlike me and unbecoming. Never has anyone seen me take my shoes off so much!' Sally attempted a joke and smiled wryly through her messy hair and blotched face as she reached down and picked up her shoes. Ruby looked at the shiny black shoes and watched her tiny reflection in them. Suddenly, it clicked!

Something that the police said to Ruby triggered a brain wave. They said, 'when someone is hiding out people often go to a person that they like or feel safe with or have a connection with in some way.' Which reminded Ruby about the affectionate way in which Lucy talked about his bootmaker. She remembered him saying, with a small chunk of pickled ginger balancing precariously from his bottom lip, that being in the boot store made him feel at home. Feel safe from the outside world and where he can just be for a moment or two.

'I think I know where Lucy is!' she cried.

Instantly, Sally jumped up from her chair and started gathering her phone and car keys. 'Well, what are we waiting for, let's go!'

They drove in tense silence, Sally's eyes on the road whilst her fingers were curled tightly around the steering wheel. Ruby had her phone out and barked occasional directions, 'next left...' Both women were eager to get there. She was already going a little too fast for Ruby's liking and thought she might somehow make them speed up their journey if she leant her torso forward up to the steering wheel.

Pulling up in front of the swanky little boutique, they leapt out of the car and rushed up to the side of the building. It was a darling store, with a forest green front and gold curly signage. The window display boasted various types of boots and shoes, mostly in black. Ruby could see what her bathroom mirror was trying to tell her: it wasn't the scrying mirror she was seeing it was the reflection of Lucy's custom-made patent boots.

Sally, still conditioned as a professional put-together woman, knocked curtly on the shop door. An older man with long grey hair and a long beard to match appeared from seemingly nowhere. He smiled graciously and unlocked the door. Ruby admired his shin-length kaftan made of fine-looking orange fabric. Ironically, his feet were bare.

'Hello ladies,' the man said warmly and invitingly. Ruby could see why Lucy liked him so much. He had an automatic aura of strength and calm about him. Not to mention safety.

'Is Lucy here?' Sally did not beat around the bush.

'Ahhh yes. He is. He's upstairs in my apartment. Please do come up. You must be Sally?' The man smiled politely again.

Lucy sat sheepishly in the corner of the bootmaker's neat apartment whilst he made everyone tea. Sally expressed her concern and regret whilst Ruby watched on from the side-lines.

'I'm just so glad that you're safe. So glad. I didn't know what happened to you. I was so worried,' Sally professed.

'Well, it was all getting a bit... much,' Lucy emphasised the last word and flicked his eyes over to Ruby.

'I know. It's all my fault,' said Sally wringing her hands in her lap.

Lucy gestured to Ruby's scalp and flicked his finger up and down. Addressing Sally, as if Ruby wasn't even in the room, he said 'what's going on with this? No wig?'

Ruby shifted uncomfortably as he carried on not directly addressing her. Ruby thought she saw him mouth to Sally, 'does she know?'

Sally shook her head vigorously and held out her hands in defence.

'No wig, Rubes?' Lucy nonchalantly nodded at Ruby's mop of hair.

'Long story. Is there something I'm missing?' she asked, innocently.

Lucy stood and picked up the tall glasses that sat between them all, making a point. Sally's was obviously only half-finished. He made his way towards the kitchen which formed half the room they were sitting in, his long floral satin robe brushing the floor behind him as he ambled. He dumped the glasses in the sink and turning back to face them, leant up against it. He took one of the glasses and filling it with water from the tap, sipped it whilst he stared over the top of it at his colleagues. The bootmaker had disappeared and seemed to be busying himself with something downstairs.

'I'm not going anywhere until we get a few things straight Sally,' Lucy's voice became firm in a way that Ruby had never heard from him before. 'Number one, if I come back to Crichton Enterprises, I want a promotion. I'll help you find another assistant but I'm getting promoted or I'm walking.'

'That's completely reasonable and I'm sorry that it hasn't happened sooner.'

Lucy looked satisfied and pulled his satin robe tighter around his narrow torso. 'And two, you tell her what's up and all cards laid out on the table,' Lucy jock nodded his chin at Ruby to make a point of who needed to be brought into whatever was orbiting the both of them and bringing them both to their knees, emotionally.

'Lucy, we can't do that. It's in the contract. We're not supposed to. It will ruin our progress.'

Lucy drained the rest of his glass and threw it into the sink with enough force that it shattered. 'Absolutely fuck the progress up the cow. I can't keep the charade any longer, Ruby doesn't deserve it. What I had to do to her has left a sour taste in my mouth and I have been sick about it for weeks. And for what? So I can stay in an assistant role when I have been nothing but loyal and overperforming at this place? Nuh uh. I'm done.'

'Oh please, Lucy.' Ruby was shocked to see Sally beg. But Sally kept on surprising her with her emotional range, especially when it came to Lucy.

'Tell her what is what and I'll consider it.' Lucy pursed his lips and bounced one shoulder up and down, daring Sally to come clean.

'Fine. I'll tell her everything and you come back to work tomorrow. Walker is going to kill me. Probably fire me but I'll ensure you get your promotion.'

'Don't you worry about Walker. I'll have a word with him too,' Lucy said cockily.

'I'm really starting to feel like I'm missing something here. What's going on?' Ruby interjected.

Lucy swam up behind Sally, placed a hand on her shoulder and nodded.

Sally searched for the words. 'Ruby, we haven't exactly been honest with you about your involvement with Crichton Enterprises. The product— ClairTech— that we've been working on for ages is so confidential because it's not exactly... ethical. I mean, in the grand scheme of things it's not terrible compared to some of the stuff that our competitors are probably working on. But it's not great.' Sally held her hands up defensively. 'Of course, we plan to put a full education plan in place and people will absolutely know what they are getting into. Once it's released. Now, however, test subjects aren't really aware that they are trialling the product.'

Ruby's eyes narrowed but she held her silence allowing Sally to continue.

'You see, you weren't hired with us as a psychic. If you read your contract properly, you were hired as a test subject.'

Ruby's face went ashen. 'Excuse me?' She looked up to Lucy whose pitying eyes confirmed it.

'It has to do with your wig,' Sally said uneasily.

Chapter 19

Chapter 19

Ruby sat alone at Cynthia's and was almost glad that it was Ana's rare night off. She wasn't sure she could face someone she knew with all the humiliation that was coursing through her veins. What a complete double down on the mortification from misinterpreting Walker's intentions and to find out that she had been used like a roll of toilet paper.

Ruby absentmindedly rubbed the back of her head where she'd been struck. By what she thought was an intruder. A stranger. But to find out it was Lucy who had broken in to her apartment and down that, it really wounded her. The betrayal felt thick through her blood as she remembered who she thought was her friend was actually someone she was terrified of. Someone that had intentionally done her harm. And for what? Company loyalty? A potential promotion?

At least he had the good sense to feel bad about it and have remorse. He apologised profusely, as did Sally but Ruby didn't know if she could ever face them again. Reading through her contract properly, that she had signed in a hurry with the fervour and excitement of starting a new job, she noticed they were right. She did inadvertently sign up to be a test subject. Little did she know that she was testing out their new technology product, ClairTech, which was a listening and audio device that was so tiny it could be hidden almost anywhere. Like, for example, inside a wig.

The warm, familiar voice that she had been hearing was, in fact, an AI-generated one that was fed through the device to tell her things that Lucy managed. To manipulate her. To think that she was psychic. It turns out that the night Ruby got home to her apartment, Lucy hadn't gotten out quick enough after he implanted the device into her wig. And he panicked and whacked her over the back of her head. He didn't intend for her to pass out for the rest of the night, he just wanted to get out unseen. A memory of seeing his shiny boots in her eye-line as she lay on the floor of her own bedroom kept flashing back. The same boots that came to her in the bathroom mirror vision that led her finding him holed up at his shoemaker friend, Edwardo's, place.

The fire? That was also ClairTech, which they quickly realised couldn't be attached to a phone headset without setting the thing on fire!

'But what we weren't counting on,' Sally said in all earnest, 'was that you really are psychic! I mean, that vision you had of me having just given birth was mind-blowing!' she said enthusiastically as Lucy gave her a queer sideways look.

Sally was right, it wasn't just the wig's audio instructions that gave her psychic abilities. For they didn't account for the visions she had, especially the ones she had without even wearing the wig. For whatever reason, the belief that she was psychic through the catalyst that was ClairTech had fuelled her actual psychic powers to life.

Ruby thought over how Sally had explained it all. 'It was fitted with a wide-reaching microphone and it really wasn't our intention to spy, initially. There are probably too many legalities around that anyway. We hadn't really settled on the final marketable use for such a product. I mean, clearly you can see a whole range of things: a communication device for people in dangerous or undercover situations, as a fashionable way to connect to loved ones, cognitive training and guidance. We just wanted to see how powerful the directives would be if we applied it to you, an unsuspecting person that had no prior knowledge of what we were up to.

'That rat eyed motherfucker,' Lucy had the decency to say after Ruby said that the wig was lost in Herman's presence after their encounter. 'Have you tried listening in?' He directed at Sally.

'Yes, the moment Ruby told me that she'd left the wig at his house. But I couldn't really hear much. I heard the police arrive at his place after his house staff called for emergency services. Turns out, Ruby threw the wig in his face and it knocked him off balance so much that he tumbled down the stairs in an alcoholic stupor.' Lucy laughed like he was new to laughing and clutched at his perfectly satin clad sides.

'Oh Ruby, this is why I couldn't continue this messed up charade. I like you too damn much,' Lucy winked at her.

Replaying the conversations in her head, her shoulders heavy and rounding over, Ruby stared into her half-drunk yellow beer as if there were answers to be found in there. Back to square one. There was no way she could go back to the horrid sneaky rat's nest that was Crichton Enterprises. After finding a job that had finally set her on a pathway to the freedom and financial security that she wanted, it had been taken away from her again. Not to mention the betrayal that she had been served up.

But Ruby let something sit within her. Although she was tempted to wallow, to fall in a heap and wonder why life was so unfair and why she was never getting anywhere despite her best efforts, she chose another path. Like a switch going off inside her, she made a decision. An empowering and forthright decision that would change the course of her life. She was no longer going to be a victim. Just like she chose when she escaped from Herman's place. Everything up until this point in her life she felt like life, especially the bad things, had happened to her. But, for once, she decided that everything, even the so-called bad, was happening for her. Not against her.

Sure, it may look absolutely messy on paper: being used as some sort of experiment, being taken advantage of by people, being assaulted not just once, but three times: once by someone she regarded as a friend. It wasn't great. But Ruby had a newfound outlook on life. A confidence stirred to life within her, an ancillary gift that her psychic talents had given her.

The time at Crichton Enterprises had been formidable enough to spur on her abilities and there was no reason why she couldn't use them elsewhere. She had escaped Herman's disgusting clutches not once but twice. Not only surviving but she felt like she could hold her own in almost any tough situation that would arise for her going forward.

One of the best parts was that she also liked the side of herself that could truly help people, like she did with Ana that night in the bar when she had an epileptic episode. It gave her great satisfaction and she knew that the opportunity would arise soon enough for it to happen again.

But most of all, she knew she had the power within her to make money now that she'd been shown what is possible. And not just make money enough to slightly boot her out of debt. But make enough money to start saving for the bookstore that she wanted. Although, as she looked around the bar at the people smiling at one another the want for the bookstore felt further and further away. It was no longer a burning desire for her. What had replaced it was to help people with her psychic gifts.

Chapter 20

Chapter 20

Floating out of the bar, with her new brighter outlook, Ruby looked up and down the street for something to catch her eye. She didn't want to go home just yet, especially because it meant that she would go to bed and sleep and the next thing she'd know it would be morning and she would have to decide what she was going to do about her job at Crichton Enterprises. Although she already knew in her heart of hearts that she wouldn't be able to continue there, not with the way they took advantage of her and the disappointing ethics they showed. Ruby never thought she'd be one for putting ethics over money but here she was.

It was still early so she took a deep breath and sauntered towards the bookstore, hoping Cooper was working the evening shift. The dregs of the light twinkled between the leaves, like it was playing peek a boo and she smiled to herself. Reaching into her bag, she rummaged around until her hand hit the pile of flyers.

Making sure she carefully and thoughtfully slid each of the Gloria's Spirit's advertisements under ever door she came across, it twigged in her that it would be just as easy to make up her own flyers and deliver them to strangers. 'Psychic for hire,' she would put. A fresh wave of enthusiasm hit her. She could also now legitimately advertise, 'can find missing people and talk to the dead.' If that wasn't a stellar advertisement for her services than what was?

Turning a familiar corner, the welcome view of the bookstore came into sight. Having not visited it since she was fired, she was extremely trepidatious. But her stomach was flooded with warmth upon spotting the chocolate brown shop and the kindly glow that emanated from within.

Flicking her eyes through the window as she tried to casually walk past, she noticed Cooper was there, bent over the desk, flicking through a small book. He smiled at her but then his face quickly dropped into nervousness when he saw her.

'Edward.' She nodded at him with fake formality.

'Rubes!'

'Just thought I'd pop in. Wait until you hear the outrageousness that has happened to me.'

'I want to hear everything. But did you get my voicemail?'

'I haven't had a chance to listen, what with basically living in some kind of episode of *Black Mirror* over here.'

Cooper sniggered unsure if he was supposed to. 'My voicemail said, basically, that I was talking to Jared— you know, that guy I dated awhile back? With the bad breath?'

Ruby nodded wide-eyed but they both knew she'd forgotten who he was.

'Anyway, he was talking to Pete who said

that he knows a guy called Lucy. And I thought... how many guys called Lucy are there? I remembered you mentioning him and for some reason he stuck in my mind. And so...' Cooper took a breath.

'Wait, who's Pete?'

'Doesn't matter,' he said waving away the question. Ruby was enjoying how unusually animated he was.

'... Pete told Jared who told me that Lucy was dating his boss! And they had to keep it all hush hush because he was the CEO and if anyone found out it would be a disaster for both of them. Do you think that's your Lucy, Ruby?'

All of a sudden, the room started to whirl around Ruby as if it were giving her a great big comforting hug. Her vision, of Walker saying that he loved her made complete sense. Her psychic senses weren't faulty at all! Walker didn't love her; Walker was in love with Lucy! It was Lucy who was standing behind her when she had the vision. He was saying he loved Lucy! Ruby's heart swelled at the thought of them as a couple, despite what they had done to her, she couldn't help but feel a fondness for them, especially together. And with the clarity that her gift was always accurate, with a hundred per cent strike-rate now, the humiliation of confronting Walker washed away. Even more so now that she wouldn't have to see them if she didn't go back.

Ruby squealed and regaled the whole story to Cooper: about the vision she had of Walker revealing his feelings and her subsequent embarrassment. Which Cooper had the good grace to pretend to not be completely amused by. And then Ruby, barely taking a breath and waving her hands around in the air, filled him in on the whole thing. Where they found Lucy, the wig and the technology and the experiment. By the end, Ruby's heart was racing so fast as the reality of it all whooshed up at her.

Cooper stared at her with his mouth agape. Ruby slightly leant her torso forward and took two fingers beneath his chin and pushed his mouth closed with a wink.

'So you're not mad at me?' Cooper asked.

'Why the heck would I be mad at you?'

'I thought you were mad at me because you

didn't return my calls. It turns out you were just playing Miss Marple all over the place.'

'It's been quite the adventure! I didn't even know I had it in me, to be honest. The best part is that the psychic stuff, well, it's all real! It's all me. Not exactly sure what I'm going to do with it just yet, that's for you and me to figure out pretty soon. Did you think I would be mad because you didn't tell me sooner about Lucy and Walker? There's no way I'd be mad about that.' Ruby was rambling as any leftover adrenalin burnt itself out within her.

'No Ruby,' Cooper reached out to take her hand but thought the better of it. 'I thought you'd be mad because of my latest purchase. Ruby, I bought this place.' He swivelled his torso as he surveyed the shelves around him, like he was looking over his bountiful land.

'Oh Cooper!' Tears inadvertently sprung up in Ruby's eyes. 'Of course, I'm not mad. That's the best news I've ever heard! I'm so happy for you. Truth be told, I'm on a new pathway now as Miss Psychic Babe of the Year. And I'm kinda over the whole idea of owning a bookstore. But for you? Yes. This is absolutely happening.'

Cooper shone like Ruby had never seen any-one light up before. His smile stretched across his face until it pushed his ears back.

'Careful now Edward, you're starting to glit-ter.'

'Cut it out,' Cooper playfully swiped at her.

'When is it officially yours?'

'The end of this week. It basically means I'm living off beans and you'll have to shout the chardonnays from now on.'

'I think I can manage that,' Ruby said earnestly. 'But I might need to do a few shifts for you.'

Cooper laughed and wiggled her name badge at her. 'Well this is still here and waiting for you anytime you want.'

The pair looked around the bookstore, both the happiest they had ever been. They moved about in silence for a little while, straightening books here and there but they were both lost in their own little worlds of bliss. Everything was going to be alright.

As Cooped shuffled Ruby out of the store and locked the door behind them both at closing time, Cooper said, 'oh, by the way, I forgot to ask. Did you get my flowers?'

The end.

The Tens

Ever since Sophie's thirtieth birthday, she has been losing sleep and having hallucinations and not a night goes by without an unexplainable reoccurring nightmare.

And then her husband leaves her out of the blue, without explanation and seems to vanish without a trace. This tips her over the edge and she realises it's time to seek therapy. At first, her soothing therapist, Carla, is everything she needs.

But when she notices a keyring that is identical to her husband's in Carla's handbag, Sophie's suspicions get the better of her and she follows her home one night. But she loses Carla midpursuit and happens upon a camp full of helpful people. A little too helpful, Sophie thinks...

The Tens is a psychological thriller that tackles the

theme of mysticism versus madness that will encourage readers to see the power is always within.

Madame Maudelynne and The New Way

Madame Maudelynne was a sought after psychic reader who joined a beloved circus in the 1860s.

After a bout of fever, she discovers something that all people must know and quickly sets about helping everyone to prepare for The New Way.

An intriguing short story for lovers of historical and occult fiction. This story forms the preface to the psychological thriller novel *The Tens* by the same author but can be read as a standalone.

Uneasy: short stories

Uneasy is a collection of dark short stories with an undercurrent of suburban ennui and the uneasiness that comes from ordinary life. Each story is haunting in its way it highlights the things we don't want to talk about but, nonetheless, exist.

Featuring a signature darkness and poetic style, whilst tackling centuries old themes that are still relevant today, such as unrequited love, deep domestic unhappiness and the desperate and misguided strive for normality.

For upcoming releases, specials and other great
reads be sure to head to:

vanessajonesauthor.com

www.ingramcontent.com/pod-product-compliance
Lightning Source LLC
Chambersburg PA
CBHW021644110726
47902CB00007B/1812